THE CIRCLE WE MADE

Abu Bakr Shareef

The Circle We Made

Copyright © 2025 by Abu Bakr Shareef

For the ones who stayed.

The ones who sat in silence.

The ones who prayed with trembling hands.

And the ones still searching for their Circle—this was always for you.

And to my brothers and sisters in faith—Mansur, Omar, Modar, Nabil, Tawfiq, Muhammad, Rasheed, Henna, Sonia, and countless more...thank you, and May Allah give you the best in this life and the next. Ameen.

Table of Contents

Acknowledgments

Alhamdulillah.

To the students who inspired this story—your questions, laughter, and fearlessness shaped every page.

To the brothers and sisters who gathered in dorm rooms, lounges, masajid, and campus lawns to pray, cry, and rebuild—your legacy is real.

To those who've ever felt too Black, too Muslim, too quiet, or too loud to belong: you were the light this book needed.

To my family—thank you for loving me unconditionally.

And to every reader who found part of themselves in these pages: may you build your own Circle, and may it always remain lit.

CHAPTER ONE

The Summer Before the Storm

Tariq's Arrival

The August sun had a cruel way of showing up on move-in day—bright and boastful, as if it too had something to prove. Tariq adjusted his baseball cap, the sweat already creeping along his hairline, and stared up at the aged stone of Hamilton Hall like it might come alive and swallow him whole. Columbia University. Ivy League. The dream. The weight.

His father's SUV idled too long in the roundabout. "You gonna stand there all day, or help us unload?" his mother called from the passenger seat, halfway through a sip of her lukewarm coffee. She wore her favorite sunglasses, the oversized ones with the tortoiseshell rims, and the expression of a woman holding in more opinions than the city had cabs.

Tariq jogged to the back of the vehicle and popped the trunk. His suitcases were stacked neatly—thanks to his twin sister Nadia, who'd spent the night before triple-checking his packing list via FaceTime from her dorm room at Howard. He could still hear her voice in his head: "Columbia's no joke, 'Riq. You need to hit the ground running. No distractions."

"Got it, Ma," he said, grabbing the first bag. His father emerged from the driver's seat slowly, in his Friday-best slacks and a short-sleeved button-down that clung to his chest with sweat. The man looked like he wanted to say something profound, but instead just nodded and headed for the dorm entrance with one of the lighter bags in hand.

The check-in table was surrounded by wide-eyed freshmen and frantic parents. The air buzzed with introductions, heavy lifting, and the bittersweet noise of independence gaining ground.

As they walked up the stone steps, his mom reached out and adjusted the collar of his polo shirt, like it was still the first day of kindergarten. "Don't forget to call your grandmother this week. She prayed for you at fajr this morning."

"I won't forget," Tariq murmured. "Tell her thank you."

"Tell her yourself," his dad chimed in. "You grown now."

There it was again—that double-edged freedom. Grown enough to make your own bed, but not enough to escape expectation.

Inside Carman Hall, the line for the elevator was backed up, so they took the stairs. Third floor. Left wing. The hallway smelled like industrial cleaner and nervous sweat.

His room was smaller than he'd imagined. Two twin beds. Two desks. Two wardrobes. No AC. He set his bags down and stood at the window. The view wasn't much—just the tops of city buildings and a sliver of the Hudson if you craned your neck. But he felt it anyway. This was his world now.

His mother handed him a small envelope with his name on it in her script. "Don't open it until we leave," she said, avoiding his eyes.

His father gave a tight, one-armed hug. "You know who you are. Don't forget."

Tariq nodded. He didn't trust his voice not to crack.

When the door finally closed behind them, the silence pressed down like the weight of everything unsaid. He sat on the edge of the bed, ripped open the envelope, and found a single line on the card: "Even prophets started with doubt. Stay steady."

He stared at it until the letters blurred. Then his phone vibrated.

Nadia: "Don't get soft on me now, Ivy Boy. Call me after you unpack."

Tariq smiled for the first time all day.

The Dorm Room Collision

Tariq was halfway through organizing his side of the room—folding clothes, lining up toiletries—when the door burst open like it had been waiting for the perfect dramatic cue.

"Ayoo, Salaam Alaikum!"

A tall, cinnamon-brown guy strode in with a beat-up Knicks duffel slung over one shoulder and a rolling carry-on in the other. His voice filled the room before his presence did. He wore a crisp vintage Knicks jersey, cargo shorts, and sneakers that looked too clean to have touched New York pavement.

"You must be the roommate. Name's Abe," he said with a grin that stretched without apology. "Well, Abdullah technically. But only people who yell at me use that name. Kuwait born, Jersey raised. Don't tell my pops I said that."

Tariq chuckled. "Tariq. Maryland."

"Ah, DMV boy. I can mess with that."

Abe dropped his bag with a dramatic sigh and surveyed the room like a real estate agent inspecting prime property. "Which bed you claim?"

"That one," Tariq said, pointing to the side closest to the closet. "Already started unpacking."

"Cool, cool," Abe nodded. "I'm a window dude anyway. Gotta have that light. Helps me wake up spiritual and all that."

He was already unzipping his duffel, revealing a loud mix of designer hoodies, off-brand snacks, and what appeared to be a portable speaker peeking out from under a Quran wrapped in cloth.

Tariq raised an eyebrow. "You really brought a speaker to college?"

3

"Bro, you want me to survive Columbia without sound? What am I, a monk?"

Before Tariq could answer, the door creaked open again. This time, the figure that entered was much quieter—taller, thinner, and moving with precise, almost deliberate care. His kufi was modest, his button-down shirt crisp and tucked in. He paused at the threshold, scanning the room and the two of them with a steady, unreadable expression.

"Alaikum Salaam," he offered, voice low and calm. "I'm Musa. From The Gambia."

Tariq extended his hand, and Musa shook it with firm politeness. No extra words, no small talk. Just presence. He moved with the kind of discipline Tariq recognized from years of Jumu'ah khutbahs but rarely saw in anyone under 40.

Musa placed his single suitcase on the empty bed and slowly began to unpack. Every shirt folded sharply. Books arranged with care. A prayer mat, clean and neatly folded, was placed at the foot of the bed. There was a discipline to it all that made the room feel... anchored.

"Man, y'all all serious," Abe mumbled, flopping back onto his bed. "I didn't even bring sheets. I figured the school would hook that up."

Tariq laughed. "You're bold."

"Or unbothered," Abe replied, tossing a bag of plantain chips toward the dresser. "Depends on who you ask."

Musa didn't react. He simply placed a tasbeeh—a string of prayer beads—on his nightstand and took a quiet seat on the edge of the bed. He glanced once at the window, then closed his eyes for a long moment. The room shifted. Not in tension, but in tone.

Then came a knock. Sharp. Rhythmic. Tariq opened the door to find a slim guy with jet-black hair, thick glasses, and a backpack that looked like it could swallow him whole.

"I heard someone say salaam earlier," he said with a tentative smile. "I'm

Michael. From Indonesia."

Abe sat up. "We collecting continents now? C'mon in, bro. You Muslim too?"

Michael nodded. "Yes. I am. I also code. And build websites. And apps. And possibly accidentally took over a student-run gaming server last semester... but that's another story."

"You had me at code," Tariq said, amused.

"Don't encourage him," Abe grinned. "We already got Musa over here making us look bad. Now we got the Jakarta tech genius. I'm feeling underachieved."

Michael gave a shy smile and took a seat at Tariq's desk, opening his laptop and glancing around like he was already scanning for outlets.

Just as they began to settle into a rhythm, the door nudged open once more—this time without a knock. A shorter guy stepped in, not quite stocky, but compact. Neat haircut. Button-down shirt, starched stiff. A leather-bound planner tucked under his arm.

"I was told this is the Muslim floor," he said, glancing around. "I'm Hasan. Bangladeshi. Grew up in Jersey. Economics major, languages minor. I speak six fluently."

"Dang," Abe said. "We already had six different accents in here. Now we got six languages too?"

"I also study real estate on the side," Hasan added. "My family owns several properties. My brother wants me to come home every weekend to manage leasing, but I told him Columbia needs my full focus."

"Translation," Abe muttered, "You're bougie with a calendar."

"I prefer efficient," Hasan shot back without flinching.

Tariq smiled. "I'm Tariq. Maryland. Undeclared."

Michael gave a small wave. Musa nodded in acknowledgment. Abe threw a plantain chip at Hasan. It missed.

Later that night, after everyone had half unpacked and the room looked like a low-budget UN summit, Abe proposed they all hit the MSA mixer the next evening.

But first," he said, pointing toward the hallway, "We gotta try that halal cart near Butler Library. I heard the lamb and rice slap."

"You just moved in. Who told you that?" Tariq asked.

"My barber. Before I left Jersey."

"That's not a reliable source."

"He's from the Bronx, bro! Don't disrespect."

Musa remained silent, but his eyes flickered open from his brief nap.

"We can eat," he said plainly, "but I will pray maghrib first. Anyone joining?"

There was a pause. Then Tariq stood. "Yeah. I'm in."

Hasan nodded. "Me too."

Michael adjusted his watch. "I set reminders. Five minutes."

Abe sighed, raising a finger. "Gimme ten. Gotta find my wudu socks."

And just like that, what began as awkward cohabitation was already softening into something else. Not quite friendship. But foundation.

As they each prepared for prayer, the city buzzed just beyond the window—horns, sirens, snippets of music from a passing car. The world was loud. But in that small dorm room on the third floor of Carman Hall, something sacred had quietly begun.

Orientation and First Mosque Visit

The following day arrived like the city itself—loud, fast, and not interested in waiting for anyone to catch up.

Orientation at Columbia was equal parts excitement and exhaustion. Lines wrapped around Low Memorial Library like concert queues. Booths lined College Walk offering everything from free iced coffee to credit card debt disguised as student perks. Upperclassmen volunteers in matching shirts shouted directions over each other. A DJ booth played a confusing mix of

Nirvana and Nas. The aroma of halal hot dogs, and high ambition danced in the air.

Tariq stood at the edge of it all, gripping his welcome folder and scanning the crowd for a familiar face. Abe had bailed five minutes into the morning schedule, claiming the orientation leaders had "cruise ship energy." Michael had followed him, muttering something about optimizing his course schedule instead of "wasting time with icebreakers." Musa was off the grid. Hasan was allegedly arguing with the bursar's office about a missing scholarship line item.

So Tariq stood alone—until he wasn't.

"You look lost," came a voice with a soft Cuban cadence.

He turned to see a girl with tawny skin, a cobalt hijab, and eyes like she'd already seen everything and still had questions. She held a clipboard, wore a Columbia MSA badge, and somehow made the oversized volunteer t-shirt look like fashion.

"I'm not lost," Tariq said, clearing his throat. "I'm... observing."

She smiled. "That your major?"

"I haven't declared."

"Then you're officially a 'Drifter.' That's what we call undecided folks."

Tariq laughed. "Thanks for the label."

"Anytime. I'm Sonya, by the way. MSA Board. If you're Muslim and new, I'm supposed to say salaam and give you this."

She handed him a flyer. It read: "MSA Kick-Off Mixer — Tonight 6:30 PM. Islamic Center of NYU. Food. Vibes. Family."

"I thought it'd be on campus," he said, scanning the address.

"We want freshmen to know the city is their campus too," Sonya replied. "Also, Columbia charges for room reservations."

"Ah, capitalism."

"Exactly. You coming?"

Tariq hesitated. "Yeah. I'll come."

"Bring your roommates. Or don't. But come."

She disappeared into the crowd as fast as she'd arrived, clipboard slicing through clusters of overwhelmed students like a scythe of competence. Tariq watched her go, still holding the flyer.

By late afternoon, the crew had reconvened back in their room—somewhat sunburned, significantly unimpressed.

"Yo, why did that RA try to get me to sign up for speed dating?" Abe asked, flinging himself onto the bed like a dramatic actor ending a monologue. "I told him, 'Do I look like I need help meeting people?'"

"You absolutely do," Hasan said without looking up from his laptop.

"I met a girl today," Tariq offered, casually. Too casually.

Abe sat up. "What?! Already? My guy, it's been like twelve hours since move-in!"

"Not like that," Tariq said, rolling his eyes. "She was running the MSA table. Gave me this."

He tossed the flyer to the center of the room. Michael picked it up.

"Islamic Center of NYU," he read aloud. "I heard their masjid is very beautiful. Designed by a Turkish architect."

"I'm down," Hasan said, still typing. "Networking is part of academic strategy."

"I'll go," Musa said simply. He'd returned from somewhere without explanation, a bottle of water in hand and that same quiet energy in his movements.

"Fine," Abe huffed. "But I'm not wearing shoes in the masjid. Y'all better not judge my socks."

By 6:00 p.m., they were on the downtown 1 train headed for Washington Square. It was the first time all six of them traveled together, and the subway car was too cramped to ignore how different they looked. Their crew felt like the beginning of a new species—Muslim and American, foreign and local, humble and bold.

Rohan hadn't joined them yet—they hadn't met him. But something in the atmosphere already hinted this was just the beginning. Tariq watched a woman across the train eye their group. She scanned Musa's kufi, Michael's modest attire, and Hasan's buttoned-up shirt. Her gaze lingered a second too long. Not angry. Just... cautious.

He looked down, annoyed by how visible they were.

"Y'all feel that?" he whispered.

Abe smirked. "Welcome to New York, bro. We're either a threat or a tourist attraction."

Michael nodded solemnly. "Sometimes both."

Musa looked unbothered. "We do not shrink."

The train screeched into the station. They emerged into the pulse of downtown—Washington Square Park alive with performers, food carts, and tourists photographing pigeons like rare birds.

The Islamic Center was tucked discreetly a few blocks away, modern yet modest. Inside, the carpet was soft and clean, the lighting warm. Already, dozens of students mingled in the open hall—sisters on one side, brothers on the other, laughter humming under the low echo of shoes being removed and greetings exchanged.

Abe headed straight for the food table. Michael followed him, already asking the volunteers about prayer app development. Tariq stood with Musa and Hasan near the wall, watching it all unfold.

That's when Sonya found him again.

"You came."

"I said I would."

"I half-expected you to ghost. A lot of new guys say they'll come then don't."

"I don't ghost," he said.

She nodded. "Good."

They stood in the awkward pause of semi-strangers with too much chemistry.

"I like this," Tariq said finally, motioning to the energy in the room.

"It's the only space we really have where nobody's asking us to explain ourselves," she said. "Enjoy it. These rooms are rare."

Then she disappeared again—always moving.

Later that evening, the brothers lined up shoulder to shoulder for prayer. Tariq stood between Hasan and Musa. Michael was in the back. Abe barely made it before takbir.

The imam's voice rolled over them like balm and thunder. Smooth. Convicting. When the prayer ended, they all sat quietly for a few moments. No one moved. The weight of the day, the meaning of the space, the fragile bond between them—it all pressed down in a beautiful, quiet way.

As they left, Musa turned to Tariq for the first time that night.

"You have a good presence," he said.

Tariq blinked. "Thanks... I think?"

"It is a compliment," Musa replied. "You listen with your face. That is rare."

Tariq wasn't sure what to say. He just nodded.

As they emerged into the city night, stars swallowed by neon, Abe raised his phone to take a selfie with the whole group.

"Caption this," he said. "MSA Mafia Takes Manhattan."

They laughed, huddled in, and the photo snapped mid-laughter—blurry, chaotic, perfect. In that single frame, they looked like a family.

But families are made of trials, too.

And New York had plenty to offer.

First Night in the City

The plan was simple. After prayer, hit Times Square. Get a slice. Maybe see if the city lived up to the hype. But nothing in New York ever stayed simple.

It started with Abe declaring himself "Subway Captain" despite having zero directional sense. He led them confidently to the wrong platform, then insisted the signage was "mad deceptive."

"Bro, the 2 train doesn't even stop at Times Square," Michael said, pointing at the map with deadpan precision. "We need the 1 to 50th, then transfer or walk."

Abe waved him off. "I don't trust maps. I trust vibes."

Musa muttered something under his breath in Wolof that made Tariq smirk. Michael caught it and replied in Indonesian. They both laughed.

Tariq exhaled through his nose, trying not to feel left out. Everyone around him bounced between languages like double Dutch. It wasn't even intentional—it was just muscle memory, cultural code-switching, inherited fluency. And he felt... grounded. American. Monolingual. It hit unexpectedly hard.

"You good?" Hasan asked beside him, noticing the shift.

"Yeah," Tariq nodded. "Just... listening."

Hasan gave a knowing smirk. "It's a multilingual flex in here. But trust, when they need sarcasm and subtle shade? That's when they need a native English speaker."

Tariq chuckled. "Bet."

They eventually found the right train. Packed like a metal can of mismatched ambition—tourists clutching cameras, locals pretending not to exist, performers dancing for attention and spare change. The city was alive, and it didn't care whether you were ready.

When they emerged above ground at 42nd Street, Times Square exploded into view. Lights. Everywhere. Giant screens pulsed with ads so big they swallowed buildings. Stores stretched endlessly—Sephora, Foot Locker, M&M World. A costumed Elmo waved aggressively at a tourist while a faux Spider-Man argued with a hot dog vendor over mustard. Music blared from nowhere and everywhere.

"Welcome to the belly of the beast," Abe grinned.

"This is insane," Tariq whispered, half in awe, half overwhelmed.

Sonya had warned him about the city being its own character. He finally understood what she meant.

They stood in the center of it all—just six young men in sneakers and growing faith, each more different than the next, soaking it in. No one spoke for a moment. They didn't need to.

"Alright," Hasan finally said, "Pizza?"

The group wandered toward a spot Abe insisted was "legendary" despite never having been there. They ended up at a 24-hour joint with sticky floors and cracked vinyl booths. The slices were massive, greasy, and exactly what they needed.

"You think there's halal pepperoni on this?" Abe asked.

"No," Musa said flatly.

"Then bismillah and vibes," Abe muttered before taking a giant bite.

Tariq watched them all from across the table. Michael quietly wiped sauce from his fingers before pulling out a mini-notebook and jotting something down with intense focus. Hasan argued with the guy behind the counter about whether the tap water was filtered. Musa sat upright, eating in silence but fully present. Abe leaned back, legs sprawled like the booth was his living room.

And then there was Tariq—somewhere in between.

"Y'all ever wonder what we'll be in four years?" he asked, half-thinking out loud.

Hasan glanced at him. "Successful. In sha Allah."

"I don't mean careers," Tariq clarified. "I mean... as people."

Abe leaned forward. "I'ma be the same. Just richer."

Musa finally spoke. "Growth is not optional. It is the mercy of Allah that we are forced to evolve."

Michael nodded. "Like version updates."

"Exactly," Musa said.

Tariq stared at his slice, unsure why he felt emotional. Maybe it was the surreal mashup of Quran and code-switching, spiritual reflections next to a pizza joint bathroom that smelled like defeat. Or maybe it was the fact that he already knew—deep down—that this moment was one of those memories that would age into legend.

"Take a picture," Abe said, reading the energy. "Group photo. C'mon."

They shuffled together in the booth. Hasan reluctantly put away his phone. Michael looked awkward but smiled. Musa didn't protest. Abe extended his arm with the front cam up. Tariq smiled last. A real one.

Snap.

And just like that, the moment was sealed.

Afterward, they walked back through the city. The night had thinned. Fewer tourists now. More sirens. A little more shadow in the alleyways.

They passed a street mural of Malcolm X and Muhammad Ali, both painted larger than life. Tariq stopped for a second, staring.

Musa slowed beside him. "Do you know what they used to call Ali?"

"Yeah," Tariq said. "The Greatest."

"No. I mean before that. When he was in the Nation. They called him a traitor. An extremist. A threat to democracy."

Tariq didn't reply.

"Everyone starts as something small," Musa said. "Misunderstood. Even doubted. Then they rise."

It was the longest thing he'd said all day. And he kept walking like he hadn't just dropped something sacred.

Back at the dorm, they collapsed into silence. The air was heavy but full of understanding.

Before bed, Tariq texted Nadia.

Tariq: "This place is wild. These dudes are even wilder. But... I think I found my tribe."

Nadia: "Good. Keep them close. And don't forget who you are."

He stared at the screen for a long moment before closing the chat.

Outside his window, the city pulsed. Unrelenting. Unapologetic.

Inside, something real was beginning to form.

Not just brotherhood. Not just faith.

But fire.

Foreshadowing 9/11

It was Sunday morning when they decided to walk downtown. Not take the train. Not grab a cab. Just walk.

"We'll never get this kind of time again," Tariq said, stretching outside the dorms, the late August breeze hinting at fall. "Classes start tomorrow. After that, it's all stress and survival."

The group, surprisingly, agreed.

They headed south from campus, through Harlem, down into Midtown. At first, they joked around—Abe doing celebrity impressions, Michael reciting random coding facts, Hasan giving unsolicited historical context for nearly every building they passed. Musa trailed near the front with quiet intensity, while Tariq hung back for a moment, watching them all move. Each of them so different. Each of them so specific. And somehow—somehow—they were becoming something bigger together.

As they neared the Financial District, the mood changed.

It was subtle.

The noise dropped a level. People seemed less performative. More rushed. More business. The buildings grew taller, shadows longer.

And then they turned a corner and saw them.

The Twin Towers.

Standing like sentinels over the city—giants of glass and steel. The sunlight bounced off them with quiet authority.

"Yo," Abe whispered. "That's crazy."

They all paused on the corner of Church Street. Tourists swarmed around them, snapping photos. Vendors sold postcards with the towers printed next to the Statue of Liberty.

"Never seen them in person," Tariq said quietly.

"They look... invincible," Michael added.

"They are not," Musa said, not unkindly. "Nothing built by man is invincible."

Hasan studied the crowd. "Every time I walk in this part of the city, I feel eyes on me."

"You always feel that?" Tariq asked.

"Not always. Just here. When I look too... Muslim."

They all stood in silence.

A woman walked by, glancing at them just a second too long. Her eyes swept Musa's kufi, then Tariq's skin, then Michael's slightly bowed head. She said nothing. But the air thickened.

"Let's keep walking," Musa said.

They passed by the base of the towers, weaving through camera flashes, briefcases, and tourists speaking every language under the sun. Tariq looked up once more, trying to memorize it. The height. The shimmer. The sheer scale of it all. Something tugged at his chest. Not fear. Not awe. Just... something he couldn't name.

As they turned the corner, Abe spoke softly. "Think anything could ever bring those down?"

No one answered.

That night, back in the dorms, they didn't talk about the towers again. But it lingered. As the others settled into their nightly rituals—Michael syncing his alarm with three time zones, Hasan wiping down every surface before bed, Musa praying beneath a soft desk lamp—Tariq sat at his desk and opened his notebook for the first time.

He wrote:

I think I'm supposed to be here. I don't know what I'm becoming yet, but it feels… bigger than me. There's something forming between us—this brotherhood, this breath of purpose. We're not just students. Not just Muslims. We're something in the making. And the world doesn't know us yet. But it will.

He closed the notebook. Slid it under his mattress. Lay back on the bed. And stared at the ceiling, just like he had on day one. Only now… he didn't feel alone.

The chapter was closing. Tomorrow, college would begin for real. But something deeper had already started. And somewhere in the distance, history was ticking louder.

Chapter Two

First Week Fractures

False Starts

The first week of classes hit like a wave—loud, cold, and unapologetic. Tariq stood in the back of his Introduction to Constitutional Law lecture, clutching a cup of coffee he didn't want and a syllabus that felt more like a threat. The professor had already made it clear that 50% of the class grade came from a single final essay—and that "coasting" wasn't just discouraged, it was impossible.

"You are at Columbia," the man had said with a raised eyebrow, adjusting his bow tie. "You will swim or you will sink. This is not a community college."

Tariq didn't flinch, but something in him recoiled. He wasn't some wide-eyed freshman who didn't understand the stakes. But still, the words clanged around in his head like warning bells.

When the class ended, he filed out into the hallway and checked his phone. Three missed calls from his dad. One from his mom. A voice note from Nadia.

Nadia: "Breathe. First week ain't supposed to feel right. You just survive it. Then build."

Tariq smiled. She always knew. But then his phone buzzed again—his dad, calling back immediately.

He stepped into a quiet corner of the academic building and answered. "Salam, Baba."

"Wa alaikum salam. How's it going?"

"Good. Just had my first class."

"Law?"

"Yeah."

"Good. Don't get distracted. Lots of noise in that city."

Tariq hesitated. "Yeah... I know."

"You're not like these other kids. You've got purpose. Don't forget that. And don't waste it."

The line clicked off a moment later. No goodbye. No softness. Just pressure disguised as belief.

Across campus, in the engineering lab, Michael was already miles ahead. He had not only finished the reading assignments—he had already rewritten one of the sample codes to be more efficient. But none of that stopped the isolation from creeping in. Everyone around him spoke in bursts of jargon he understood but didn't feel part of. Study groups formed like cliques in a middle school cafeteria. No one invited him.

He didn't mind. He preferred solitude. But he noticed.

During lunch, he sat on the lawn near Low Library, watching students move in curated clusters. Laptops. Podcasts. Debate club flyers. All spinning in the same orbit of self-importance.

He took out his own notebook, a lined black journal he reserved for thoughts not meant for code.

> *Note to self: Intelligence ≠ elonging. Keep coding. Keep moving. Let the silence protect you.*

He slid the notebook back into his bag and checked his email. Another offer from a startup. He deleted it without opening it.

In the business school wing, Rohan had finally arrived on campus that morning—late thanks to a "visa glitch" he blamed on Columbia's sluggish admin. He rolled in wearing a pale blue linen shirt and designer loafers, dragging a suitcase behind him that cost more than most people's tuition books. He scanned the halls like a prince returning from exile.

Rohan was precision in motion. Even jetlag didn't slow him. He already had three meetings lined up—with professors, student clubs, and one investment rep his father insisted he "drop in on." But what he didn't expect was the subtle chill. He walked into his first seminar—International Business Ethics—and immediately felt it. Eyes. Subtle. But real.

He took the only seat left: between two white students who gave him polite, clipped nods and returned to their conversations like he didn't exist. He tried to insert a comment during the discussion. The professor acknowledged it with a nod, then pivoted quickly to another student. Rohan stared at the table. For the first time since he'd stepped on American soil, he felt... irrelevant.

Back in Carman Hall, Musa sat cross-legged on his prayer rug, eyes closed, the buzz of campus life dulled behind the closed door. He had completed all of his readings. Rewritten his class schedule to prioritize theology over general electives. Avoided all dining hall meat. Refused to engage in small talk with anyone who spoke during adhan. And yet... he felt fractured.

America was loud. It pulled at the edges of his discipline like static electricity—harmless at first, but annoying in its persistence. Every billboard, every overheard conversation, every hint of distraction felt like a micro-assault on his identity.

He checked his phone. A message from his oldest sister in Banjul: "Have you sent money yet? Father needs medicine. Mama is worried." He stared at the screen, jaw tight.

He had barely been here a week. He hadn't even received his campus job assignment yet. But to them, he was already The One. The Saviour. The Scholar in America.

He turned off his phone, stood, and whispered a du'a into the quiet.

That evening, the dorm room was quieter than usual. Everyone was there, but no one was speaking much. Michael was typing. Hasan was rereading a textbook on macroeconomics. Abe sat with headphones on, nodding to something no one else could hear. Musa was folding laundry with silent reverence. Tariq stood by the window, looking out over the courtyard.

It hit him all at once—how fragile it all was. They had only just met. But already the pressure, the silence, the expectations, the disappointments were carving lines into their armor.

He broke the stillness.

"We good?"

Hasan looked up. "Define good."

"I mean... is this what y'all expected?"

"Honestly?" Abe pulled off his headphones. "I thought college would be more... free."

"It is," Michael said, still typing. "But freedom costs bandwidth."

"Facts," Hasan muttered. "I feel like I've aged ten years in five days."

"No one warned us," Musa added, voice steady. "They only told us to prepare. They didn't tell us how to endure."

Tariq nodded.

"Yeah," he said. "And the hardest part isn't the classes. It's trying to hold onto who you are when nobody cares who you were."

They all sat with that.

No solutions. No du'as or jokes this time.

Just the truth.

Faith on Campus

By Friday morning, the struggle was no longer theoretical. Tariq sat in his second lecture of the day, his leg bouncing, eyes fixed on the wall clock above the whiteboard. The professor was mid-rant about constitutional interpretation, his voice more dramatic than necessary—like every sentence should end with applause. Tariq wasn't clapping. He was calculating.

Jumu'ah prayer started at 1:15. It was already 12:48. The masjid near campus was fifteen minutes away on foot—ten if he jogged, but that meant skipping the last part of the lecture and possibly offending a professor who had already made it clear he didn't believe in "concessions for faith-based truancy." He kept looking at the clock. The seconds started to sound like a heartbeat.

Across campus, Hasan faced the same dilemma. He had just finished an econ discussion group and was walking fast—briefcase in one hand, folded prayer mat in the other. The crowd of students thinned as he made his way toward 125th Street. A few blocks later, he arrived at Masjid Malcolm Shabazz just as the call to prayer echoed down Lenox Avenue. The sound stopped him cold.

It wasn't the muezzin's voice—it was what it did to the sidewalk. People paused. Eyes lifted. Car horns softened. For a moment, even Harlem seemed to breathe in sync. Inside, the masjid was buzzing—locals, professors, students, immigrants, elders. Hasan slipped his shoes off, entered the prayer hall, and found a space between a man in hospital scrubs and an elderly West African uncle with prayer beads coiled around his wrist. For a moment, everything outside of that space fell away.

Musa had already arrived half an hour early. As always. He had walked across campus with earbuds in, not for music, but for Quran recitation. He liked to fill the gap between dunya and deen with something protective. Something holy. He had offered to meet the others, but no one had responded. He didn't take it personally. He never did. But he noticed.

Inside the masjid, he helped set up extra rows of prayer rugs. He folded coats, greeted elders, and recited quietly while waiting for the khateeb to ascend the minbar. He was early not out of fear, but love. For him, prayer wasn't just obligation—it was home.

Abe didn't make it. He meant to. Swore up and down he would. But the night before, he had stayed up watching stand-up comedy specials and debating conspiracy theories with two guys from another floor until 3 a.m. He woke up late, groggy, and confused about which way was qibla. By the time he pulled on jeans and checked the time, it was already 1:24.

He stood in the middle of the room, one sock on, heart pounding with shame. He could have gone. He could've skipped the shower. Could've jogged the whole way. But instead… he sat down on his bed. "Next week," he muttered. And yet, the guilt clung to him like morning breath.

Michael did go. But he stayed in the back. He always stayed in the back. It wasn't that he didn't believe. He did. Quietly. With logic and reverence. But the masjid made him anxious. The way people looked at his shoes. The way his awkward Arabic stood out during salah. The subtle side-eyes when he made wudu too slowly.

He had memorized every surah that began with alif-laam-meem but forgot how to relax in spiritual space. He wondered if he was "too modern" for tradition—or too religious to fully blend in with the tech crowd he belonged to. He sat on the carpet, back straight, eyes fixed forward. He prayed with the rest. Said ameen. Nodded at the khutbah. But he didn't feel… part of it. Not yet.

Tariq made it just in time. He had bolted the moment class ended, ignoring the professor's glare as he grabbed his bag and muttered a rushed "sorry." He ran through the quad, darted down Broadway, and arrived just as the first takbir echoed through the building. He found a spot near the back, breathless, slightly embarrassed at how sweaty he was.

And yet—when the rows straightened, and the imam's voice rose, something inside him stilled. He thought about his dad's voice. About the disappointment laced into every phone call. About the pressure to be successful, to be elite, to be "the example." And here he was, one of dozens kneeling shoulder-to-shoulder with janitors, doctors, cab drivers, professors. No one cared about GPA. No one asked for résumés. In this space, he was just... a believer. And that was enough.

After prayer, they met outside. The sun was hot, but the sidewalk was full of peace. Musa stood waiting, arms folded. Hasan was adjusting his satchel. Tariq approached them first, then Michael.

"Where's Abe?" Hasan asked.

Michael glanced down. "Didn't come."

They stood quietly for a moment. The absence was louder than the presence.

Then Abe came running around the corner, slightly out of breath.

"Too late?" he asked, eyes wide.

"Finished ten minutes ago," Tariq said.

Abe dropped his head. "Damn. I really tried. I got up late and then I—"

Musa raised a hand gently. "No need for excuses. Next week, insha'Allah."

Abe nodded. "Yeah. Next week."

They walked back toward campus in pairs—Tariq and Abe trailing behind, Hasan and Michael deep in conversation about their dorm kitchen's broken microwave, and Musa quietly making dhikr with his fingers.

"You ever feel like it's hard to keep up?" Abe asked softly.

"With prayer?"

"With all of it. Faith. School. Identity. Like... I'm tryna be a good Muslim, but I'm also just tryna survive out here. There's so much... pressure."

Tariq exhaled. "Yeah. I feel that. Every day."

Abe nodded. "My parents expect me to wild out. But I don't want to be a stereotype, man. I wanna be solid. I just don't always know how."

Tariq looked ahead, watching the others. "You don't have to be perfect," he said. "Just consistent. And honest."

Abe cracked a small smile. "That sounds like something you tell yourself too.

"It is," Tariq said. "Every morning."

That night, Musa wrote in his journal. One sentence.

> *Faith is not a fortress. It is a fire. You feed it, or you watch it go out.*

He closed the book, performed wudu, and went to sleep. The city buzzed outside. Lights blinking. Horns distant. Sirens slicing silence. And within the chaos, six young men searched—each in their own way—for what it meant to be faithful, flawed, and still rising.

Cultures in Collision

It started over takeout. One paper bag. Six men. Too many opinions.

Hasan had just returned from a South Asian cultural mixer with a feast of leftovers: biryani, naan, chicken curry, chickpeas, and something spicy enough to start a fire in the Bronx. He dumped it all onto the dorm's communal table like a declaration. "I'm not letting this go to waste," he said. "Grab a plate."

Michael, who hadn't eaten all day, was the first to dig in. Abe followed, balancing a paper plate like it was a trophy.

Musa, however, stood still—arms crossed. "This is zabiha?" he asked flatly.

Hasan paused, mouth half-full. "It's from a Pakistani place on 6th. They said the meat's halal."

Musa raised an eyebrow. "Said. Not verified."

"Bro." Abe wiped his mouth. "Here we go."

"I'm serious," Musa said. "People lie. Or don't understand. Halal isn't a label. It's a process."

"Okay, but we're not in the Middle East," Hasan said. "You expect me to trace every chicken's lineage?"

"If you claim it's halal," Musa replied calmly, "then yes."

Michael looked between them, chewing slower. Tariq leaned back in his chair. He'd seen sparks before. But this? This was different. It wasn't about food. This was about something deeper.

"Let's just cool it," Tariq offered. "We all trying to do our best out here."

Musa looked at him. "That is the problem. 'Trying' has replaced 'doing.' You all say bismillah and hope for the best. That is not deen. That is convenience."

"Convenience?" Hasan stood up now, offended. "Easy for you to say. You're not balancing two majors and a part-time job. You don't have professors breathing down your neck every day."

"You think I don't work?" Musa said, eyes narrowing. "I send money home. Every week. My family is depending on me to keep the lights on."

"Yeah?" Abe cut in. "Well, my family thinks I'm just here to party. They barely take me seriously. But you don't see me throwing religion in their face every five minutes."

Musa didn't flinch, but his voice went low. "Because you don't take it seriously either."

Silence. Even Michael stopped chewing.

Abe stepped forward, jaw clenched. "Say that again."

"No," Tariq said quickly, stepping between them. "He won't. And you won't ask him to. Not like that."

The air in the room had changed. It was heavy. Charged. A line had been crossed, but no one wanted to be the first to admit it.

Hasan sat down again, breathing hard. "We're all fighting something. Don't pretend your struggle is the only one."

"Exactly," Michael added softly. "We should be learning from each other, not measuring pain like currency."

Musa said nothing. He stared out the window, eyes distant.

Tariq broke the silence. "Listen," he said, voice low. "We're not the same. We weren't supposed to be. That's the whole point. If you put six people from six different cultures in a room, it's gonna get messy. That's not failure. That's family."

Abe scoffed. "Family fights."

"Yeah," Tariq said. "And real ones stay in the room after."

They all sat in that for a while. The biryani had gone cold. The room smelled like spice and silence.

Finally, Musa stood. "I'm going to the masjid," he said, grabbing his prayer mat.

No one stopped him. He opened the door, paused, then looked back. "I am trying, too." And then he was gone.

Later that night, the tension still lingered like humidity. Abe had his headphones back on but wasn't really listening to anything. Hasan was on his laptop, aggressively typing but clearly distracted. Michael paced in small circles, whispering code into his phone for a project no one else understood.

Tariq sat with his journal open, blank page staring back. He couldn't write. Not yet. Instead, he walked out into the hall and called Nadia.

She answered on the third ring, voice warm and alert. "What's up, twin?"

"Rough night," he said, leaning against the cool wall.

"What happened?"

He told her everything. The argument. The way Musa's words stung. The look on Abe's face. The fire behind Hasan's voice. The quiet ache of it all.

When he finished, Nadia didn't speak right away. Then she said: "That's the cost of building something real. You're not here to be comfortable. You're here to learn who people are when they're cracked open. And who you are when you stand in the middle of it."

Tariq exhaled. "You always do this."

"Do what?"

"Remind me that the hard stuff is the real stuff."

"Duh," she laughed. "Now go back in that room and make sure y'all don't implode. You got a movement to build."

He chuckled. "A movement?"

"I'm just saying," she said. "These boys? They're the story."

Back in the dorm, he found Abe sitting on the windowsill.

"Couldn't sleep," Abe said. "You ever just... feel like none of this makes sense?"

"All the time."

"I'm trying, man. But it's like... I don't know what kind of Muslim I'm supposed to be."

"Maybe you're supposed to figure that out with us. Not before us."

Abe nodded slowly. "Think Musa's coming back?"

Tariq smiled. "He always comes back."

And he would. Because beneath all the clashing accents, clashing faith practices, clashing expectations, there was something magnetic pulling them together. A rhythm they hadn't quite mastered. But were learning to move in. One misstep at a time.

Lines in the Sand

It was supposed to be just a class discussion.

Tariq sat in the front row of his "Foundations of Justice" seminar, notebook open, pen poised, trying to look alert. The class was taught by a well-respected professor known for his progressive ideals—Harvard-educated, NPR-featured, and proudly atheist. Today's topic: profiling, national security, and religious extremism.

"I want someone," the professor said, hands clasped theatrically behind his back, "to defend the Patriot Act."

Silence.

Then, from the back row, a tall student with a Manhattan prep school accent cleared his throat. "I mean, look, if we're being real—after 9/11, the government had to do something. You can't just let people in kufis walk around unchecked. That's just naive."

A few students nodded. A few shifted in their seats. No one spoke.

Tariq's hand rose slowly. "Respectfully," he said, trying to keep his voice steady, "you're talking about profiling based on appearance. Which means you're saying I deserve to be investigated—without cause—because I wear a beard. Or pray. Or say salaam to my friends."

"I didn't mean you specifically," the student shot back.

"But that's the thing," Tariq said. "You did. You just don't know it."

The professor didn't intervene. No one else did either.

After class, the student passed by Tariq and muttered, "Don't take it personal, man. Just a debate."

Tariq walked out in silence. But it felt personal. Every syllable.

Musa had skipped class entirely. Not out of laziness, but necessity. He had received a call that morning from his uncle in Banjul. His father's leg wound had worsened. The hospital refused treatment without full payment. The bill had doubled. And the community was already stretched thin. They needed him. Now.

He sat in Butler Library, laptop open, job portal blinking on the screen. He had already applied to six on-campus positions—library aide, cafeteria assistant, grounds crew, mailroom clerk. But his work-study clearance was still pending. And his last email had gone unanswered. He tapped his tasbeeh beads on the desk.

This wasn't what he imagined. Not when he earned that scholarship. Not when the village gathered around and prayed over his plane ticket. Not when his mother whispered, "Make us proud." He was supposed to be thriving. Instead, he was choosing between textbooks and remittance. Between Qur'an memorization and financial desperation. He didn't want pity. But he wanted ease. Just once.

Abe stood in the middle of the quad, phone pressed to his ear, trying not to cry. "Ma, I said I'm doing okay."

Her voice was sharp and sarcastic. "You don't call. You don't text. You only remember us when you need something."

"That's not true."

"Your father says he saw your Instagram. Why are you posting prayer quotes like you're a shaykh now?"

Abe closed his eyes. "It's just a caption, Ma."

"You go to Columbia to become a poet? Or to get a degree?"

He didn't answer.

"You think you're better than us now?" she continued. "You think because you're in America, you get to choose who you are?"

He wanted to scream. Wanted to throw the phone. Wanted to run. Instead, he ended the call and sat on a bench near the sundial. The call lasted six minutes. He stared at his shoes for twenty more.

He hadn't prayed dhuhr. Not because he didn't want to. Because he felt unworthy.

Michael sat alone in a computer lab off Amsterdam Avenue. It was his favorite hiding place—cold, sterile, humming with the low comfort of hard drives spinning. He scrolled through an online forum where other Muslim coders discussed halal cryptocurrency options. He posted a question, waited for a reply, refreshed. Nothing.

His inbox blinked. Another internship offer. Six figures. Stock options. Remote. He archived it without reading it. He didn't want money right now. He wanted meaning.

He missed home. Not because of family—his parents were kind but distant. Not because of food—he cooked better than the dining hall anyway. But because back home, he belonged. Here, he was either invisible or exotic. Neither felt like home.

Later that evening, they all ended up in the dorm lounge—not by plan, but by gravity. No one said much at first. Musa was reading, but not really. Hasan scrolled his phone with a clenched jaw. Abe sat with his hoodie pulled over his head like armor. Michael was typing code so aggressively that his laptop fans kicked into overdrive. Tariq stood by the window again, arms crossed, chewing on the inside of his cheek.

He spoke first. "I got profiled in class today."

Heads turned.

"White dude said Muslims should be 'watched.' Said kufis are a red flag. And the professor just... let it happen."

Musa closed his book. Abe sat up straighter. Hasan stopped scrolling. Michael looked over the edge of his laptop screen.

Tariq swallowed. "And I realized... we can't do this alone."

No one spoke.

Then Abe said, "My mom basically told me I'm fake Muslim now."

Musa nodded slowly. "My father may lose his leg. They're waiting on my money."

Michael added, "I don't talk to anyone all day unless it's code or class."

Hasan sighed. "Sometimes I feel like we're all pretending."

And there it was. Laid bare. No posturing. No ego. Just pain. Real. Messy. Shared.

Tariq sat down on the floor. "We need each other," he said. "Like... need. Not for food. Or study groups. For this. The space to be broken. To be real."

Musa looked up. "Then let's build it."

"Build what?" Abe asked.

"A space. A brotherhood. Something that doesn't disappear when class ends or the semester gets hard."

Hasan nodded. "An anchor."

Michael whispered, "A firewall."

Tariq smiled. "A circle."

They all looked at each other. Different skin. Different accents. Different scars.

But something was rising between them. Not perfection. Not agreement. But intention.

The line had been drawn. Not between them—but around them. They would stumble. Argue. Fall short.

But they would hold. Together.

Foundation Laid

The idea wasn't planned. It never is when it's real.

It was past midnight, and the dorm had settled into its usual hum—soft laughter from other floors, music leaking under doors, the occasional toilet flush breaking the silence like a drumbeat.

Tariq sat at his desk with the lights off, staring at the empty space between his bed and Musa's. He wasn't thinking about tomorrow's assignments. Or his father's voice. Or even the student who reduced his faith to a threat.

He was thinking about what Musa said earlier.

"Then let's build it."

Not a club. Not a group chat. Not a social media movement.

A circle. A space.

He stood up, stretched, then quietly knocked on each door. "Prayer. Now. Our room."

He didn't explain. He didn't need to. They came. One by one.

Musa arrived first, prayer mat folded clean as always, and placed it facing east. Then came Hasan, rolling his sleeves, hair still damp from a late-night shower.

Michael entered next—barefoot, blinking like he had just woken from a code-induced trance. He carried nothing but sincerity.

Abe came last, hesitation in his posture, headphones still around his neck. He didn't speak. Just nodded.

Tariq stood at the center, adjusting the blinds so the city lights glowed just enough to guide them.

They didn't say a word. They didn't debate over who would lead.

Musa stepped forward. They lined up.

Six young men. No imam. No masjid. No Friday requirement.

Just a decision. To pray. Together. Shoulder to shoulder. Backs straight. Hearts trembling.

The takbir rose from Musa's lips—calm, steady, soft enough not to disturb the rest of the dorm, but strong enough to shift something eternal.

"Allahu Akbar."

God is Greater.

Greater than deadlines.

Greater than shame.

Greater than debt and doubt and disconnect.

Greater than silence.

Greater than the fear that maybe, just maybe, they weren't good enough.

They moved through the motions—each takbir a thread, each sajdah a cleansing. For once, no one was rushing. No one was watching. No one was performing.

It was raw. Pure. Heavy with something holy.

And when the final salam was whispered, the room didn't erupt into discussion or awkward jokes. They just sat there. In silence. Letting it settle. Letting it sanctify the space.

Musa folded the prayer mat. Michael picked at the fraying corner of his sleeve. Hasan wiped a tear so quickly that no one noticed—except Tariq.

Abe stood, then sat back down again, as if unsure what posture faith demanded next.

Tariq looked around the room. These weren't just roommates. Weren't just classmates. They were witnesses.

To each other's struggle. To each other's becoming. To something greater than what any of them could carry alone.

He broke the silence with a whisper. "We do this every week."

Musa nodded. "Every week."

Abe added, "Maybe more."

Michael said, "Whenever we forget who we are."

Hasan looked around. "Then... we remind each other."

No one said ameen. But it was felt.

The door stayed unlocked that night. Not out of negligence. But trust.

And as each of them drifted off to sleep, the city roared beneath them—trains thundering, sirens calling, lights flashing like signals from a future still unknown.

But within the four walls of their dorm, something sacred had been built. Not a masjid. Not a movement. But a foundation. Unseen by the world. Yet unshakable.

CHAPTER THREE

New Names, Old Wounds

Her Name Was Sonya

It started with a DM. Short. Friendly. Not flirtatious. But with just enough warmth to leave the door cracked.

Sonya: "You made it through Week One. That's worth at least a halal smoothie. You in?"

Tariq stared at his phone for a full minute before replying.

Tariq: "Only if I can pay this time."

She responded with a thumbs-up and a location drop: Juice Generation, Amsterdam and 72nd. Saturday. Noon.

He checked the time. He had twelve hours to figure out how not to overthink everything.

When she walked in the next day, everything else dimmed. Not because she was the most beautiful woman in the world—though she might've been—but because she walked like she belonged. Not just in the space. In herself. Every step was quiet confidence. Her curls peeked out from under a loosely tied scarf. Gold hoops, simple but defiant, caught the sunlight.

"Thought you might ghost," she said, sliding into the seat across from him.

Tariq grinned. "I'm too Muslim to ghost. We don't disappear, we just fade until the next prayer."

She laughed. "Okay, that was smooth. I'll give you that."

They ordered: mango-spinach smoothies for both, plus two protein bars neither of them finished. The shop was mostly empty, save for a pair of grad students arguing about bioethics near the window.

"So," Sonya said, pulling out her phone, "you've survived the Ivy machine. How's it treating you?"

Tariq leaned back. "Honestly? Like it's trying to mold me into something I'm not. But I'm fighting back."

She raised an eyebrow. "And what are you?"

He paused. The question hit harder than expected.

"Still figuring that out."

"Good answer," she said. "People who think they know who they are at eighteen usually don't. They just memorize someone else's blueprint."

He studied her. "You talk like you've done this before."

"I've lived in three cities, four countries, and two realities," she said, sipping her smoothie. "My dad's Cuban, my mom's Malaysian. I grew up mostly in Miami. Dad left when I was eight. Mom found Islam through a sister's circle at a community center in Little Havana. So yeah. I've learned to shapeshift."

Tariq nodded slowly. "That explains a lot."

"Like what?"

"You walk like a woman who's carrying the weight of two names."

Sonya blinked. Then smiled. A soft one. The kind that hides a storm.

"That might be the truest thing anyone's said to me in a while."

Back at the dorm, the group had noticed.

"You got a pep in your step," Abe said, peering at Tariq like a suspect.

"It's the protein bar," Tariq said, tossing his keys onto the desk.

"Lies," Hasan called from the corner. "Your whole spirit changed."

"Chill, man," Tariq laughed. "It was just a smoothie."

"Smoothie and...?" Michael asked without looking up from his laptop.

Tariq raised his hands. "Nothing else. Conversation. That's all."

Musa glanced up from his book. "Be careful."

Tariq turned. "Of what?"

"Of becoming someone else while trying to impress someone else."

The room fell silent for a moment.

Then Abe clapped his hands once. "Welp. There it is. Musa, dropping bars."

"Seriously though," Hasan added, "She's cool. But don't lose yourself, bro."

"I'm not," Tariq said. "I just... like talking to her."

Michael nodded. "Talking is how empires fall."

Everyone turned to him.

He shrugged. "I meant that as a compliment. Kind of."

Later that night, Tariq texted Sonya again.

Tariq: "Thanks for today. For real. You're good people."

She responded.

Sonya: "You're good too. But I already knew that. Just didn't know how much."

He stared at the screen, thumb hovering over a dozen possible replies.

But he said nothing more.

Sometimes silence was the most honest language he knew.

Between Brotherhood and Boundaries

Rohan arrived like someone who'd been watching the movie from backstage, waiting for the perfect entrance. He stood in the dorm doorway midweek, a tailored backpack slung over one shoulder, polished shoes untouched by city grime, and an expression like he already knew everyone's secrets.

"Which one of you is Tariq?"

Tariq looked up from his desk. "That'd be me."

"I'm your new suite-mate. Transfer from Furnald. They overbooked international housing again. Typical." He extended a hand. Tariq shook it.

"Rohan Siddiqui," he said, as if the name should mean something. "Pakistan. Business track. Mango dynasty."

Abe, sprawled across the common room couch, perked up. "Hold up— you're the mango guy?"

Rohan raised an eyebrow. "Among other things."

Michael, who had looked up briefly, nodded and returned to his screen. Hasan was already standing, clearly intrigued. "Welcome to the madhouse," he said, offering a fist bump.

Rohan took it with a small smile. "Pleasure."

Then his eyes landed on Musa—who offered only a nod. No smile. No movement. Just watchfulness. Something unspoken passed between them.

It didn't take long for Rohan to blend in. By Thursday, he was already organizing shared supply lists, fixing the broken doorknob on the closet, and reordering everyone's laundry schedules to "maximize detergent efficiency."

"You're intense," Abe said one morning.

"I'm organized," Rohan corrected. "There's a difference."

By Friday, they found themselves sharing their first full dinner as a group—eating halal Chinese food on mismatched plates, sitting cross-legged in the common room like a patchwork tribe.

Sonya showed up twenty minutes in. Not as a surprise. Not with fanfare. Just... appeared. Tariq had invited her earlier that day—casually, quietly. No one objected. But no one confirmed either.

"Hope I'm not crashing," she said, balancing a bag of extra dumplings and homemade maduros.

Musa's face didn't change. But his body language did—slightly tighter, straighter.

"Not at all," Tariq said, standing to take the food. "You saved the night.

Abe ordered three meals for himself and claimed they were all for the group."

Sonya laughed and sat near the window, unwrapping containers like she'd done this before.

Rohan watched her closely. Not rudely. Not possessively. Just... attentively. He asked about her major. Her background. Her career goals. She answered with the same mix of candor and charm she gave everyone else— but the dynamic shifted. The group's rhythm, once loose and balanced, grew subtly skewed.

Conversations forked into sub-groups. Tariq and Sonya joked in the corner. Rohan jumped in often—maybe too often. Hasan stayed mostly quiet. Musa didn't eat much. Michael observed everything and said nothing.

At one point, Musa stood up mid-meal and walked to the kitchen. Tariq followed him after a minute.

"You good?"

Musa rinsed a plate without looking up. "She is... bold."

Tariq frowned. "That a bad thing?"

"No. Just... different."

"Different from what?"

"From the women I was taught to respect."

The words were soft. Not sharp. Not judgmental. Just true.

Tariq nodded slowly. "She's not disrespecting anything."

"I didn't say she was," Musa replied.

There was a pause.

"I just know how this goes," Musa added. "How brothers start moving different when there's a sister in the room."

Tariq swallowed. "You think I'm moving different?"

"I think we all are."

Back in the main room, Abe leaned over to Michael. "Yo. Is it just me, or is Tariq... extra?"

Michael didn't respond immediately.

Then: "He's human."

Abe raised an eyebrow. "That's your code for what?"

"Code for: let him figure it out."

Abe sighed. "Yeah, well, he better figure fast. Rohan's acting like he's auditioning for something."

Michael looked across the room at Rohan—who was mid-story about his family's mango farm turning a profit during a flood year.

And Sonya? She was smiling. Not just politely. Smiling like she saw something deeper than business plans and button-downs.

Later, after Sonya left and the containers were cleared, the room returned to something like normal. But the current was different.

Tariq lay on his bed, staring at the ceiling. Musa prayed in the corner—silent, steady. Rohan typed notes for his business ethics class, his screen glowing a faint blue.

No one spoke of Sonya. But they were all thinking about her.

Not because of love. Not because of lust. But because her presence disrupted the balance.

She reminded them of something unspoken: that they were not just students, not just brothers—but young men still learning how to be whole, disciplined, and seen.

And the line between admiration and competition was thin. Almost invisible.

Rohan's Lineage, Tariq's Dilemma

It started with a walk. Late Sunday night. No destination. Just motion. Tariq had been pacing in the dorm when Rohan, still dressed like he was heading to a networking mixer, looked up from his desk and said, "Let's go."

"Go where?"

"Does it matter?"

They walked south down Broadway, passing shuttered bodegas and flickering traffic lights, their footsteps echoing off brownstone steps and empty streets.

For a while, they said nothing. Just two young men in Columbia hoodies walking through Harlem, trying to outpace whatever was clawing at their peace. Then Rohan broke the silence.

"You like her."

Tariq didn't ask who. He didn't need to. He kept his eyes forward. "What gave it away?"

"You smile different when she texts. And you watch her when she's not looking."

Tariq chuckled dryly. "Is that a crime now?"

Rohan shook his head. "No. Just... complicated."

Tariq stopped walking. "Why?"

Rohan stopped too. "Because my family would never allow it."

The words hit like cold rain.

Tariq turned slowly. "Allow what? You dating her?"

Rohan's eyes didn't waver. "Me marrying anyone outside our circle. Outside our caste. Outside... South Asia."

The unspoken hung in the air.

Outside our race.

Tariq took a breath. "You think she'd even say yes to you?"

Rohan's jaw tightened. "That's not the point."

"What is the point?"

Rohan looked up at the city sky—choked with light, starless.

"The point is... some of us don't get to want what we want. Not out loud."

Tariq folded his arms. "And some of us were never allowed to want anything in the first place."

Rohan turned toward him. "This isn't about you being Black, bro."

"But it always is," Tariq replied, eyes steady. "Even when it's not spoken.

Even when it's dressed up in caste or tradition or class. It's always there."

Rohan didn't argue. Because he couldn't. And that silence said more than any rebuttal ever could.

Back in the dorm, Tariq sat alone at his desk, phone in his hand, thumb hovering over Sonya's name. He didn't text her. Didn't want to bring her into the weight of it all. She was light, intention, clarity. This was something heavier. He stared at his own reflection in the darkened laptop screen.

All week, he'd felt seen by her. Now, he was wondering if the world she moved through would ever let her see him fully. Not just as a friend. But as something more.

The next day, they crossed paths again. On campus. Near Low Steps. She was sitting on the edge of the fountain, legs tucked under, notebook open.

He stopped.

"Hey," she said, looking up. "You disappeared."

"Just been... processing."

She tilted her head. "Something I said?"

"No. Something I heard."

She waited.

Tariq sat beside her. "If I ever acted like I wanted something more than what we've had... I didn't mean to make things complicated."

Sonya didn't flinch. "It's only complicated if you're pretending it's not there."

He looked at her. Really looked. And in that moment, he saw the whole picture—her laughter, her confidence, her ache for belonging, her quiet loneliness tucked behind witty comebacks.

He wanted to reach for her hand. Instead, he said, "Some people won't get it. Us. They'll call it haram. Or weird. Or too much."

She smiled. "You think that's new for me?"

"No," he said. "But it's new for me. Caring this much."

She closed her notebook. "So what now?"

Tariq didn't answer. Because he didn't know.

That night, Musa noticed Tariq skipping maghrib prayer. Didn't comment. But he noticed. Abe noticed him skipping dinner, too. Hasan watched him ignore three group texts. Michael, who noticed everything, simply opened his notes app and wrote:

> *When you fall for someone while carrying a wound you haven't named— You don't land in love. You land in limbo.*

Fault Lines

It was supposed to be a night of unity. The MSA's theme: "Brothers in Faith: Building a Bond Beyond Borders."

The flyer had pictures of globes, calligraphy, and a Black silhouette shaking hands with a brown silhouette beneath a shared crescent moon. It was ambitious. Overly idealistic. A little cheesy.

But everyone came anyway.

The hall was packed—plastic chairs in perfect rows, blue-taped signs for "Sisters" and "Brothers," and samosas that went cold thirty minutes into the program. Students of every background filled the room—white converts, Arab pre-meds, Afro-Caribbean grad students, Desi undergrads in varsity jackets, East African girls with matching hijabs, and a few curious non-Muslims scribbling notes for comparative religion papers.

Tariq sat with the crew near the front.

Rohan wore his usual precision—a crisp button-down and a prayer cap he adjusted every ten minutes.

Musa was in a plain thobe, eyes locked forward like a soldier at attention.

Hasan scrolled through the program booklet.

Michael quietly reviewed the Quran app he'd helped debug last week.

Abe balanced a plate of snacks on his lap like it was an art form.

Tariq had been tense since arrival. And he wasn't the only one.

The first speaker—an older Arab imam with a flowing beard—talked about "brotherhood in the Prophet's time." His tone was measured, poetic, and vague. Lots of Arabic, not much reality.

The second speaker—an energetic convert from Harlem—shook the room awake. Spoke of racism in the Muslim community, of disunity, of being passed over for marriage because of melanin.

People clapped. Some didn't.

Rohan didn't move.

Musa closed his eyes, lips moving in silent dhikr.

Abe stopped chewing.

Tariq's jaw clenched.

Then came the panel. A sister moderated, three brothers shared mics. A Pakistani. A Somali. A Black convert from the Bronx.

The question: "What's the biggest challenge facing young Muslim men in America today?"

The Somali brother answered first—talking about pressure from back home, expectations to send money, carry legacy, marry early.

The Pakistani brother followed, discussing Islamophobia, job discrimination, the burden of always having to prove you're not a threat.

Then the brother from the Bronx took the mic.

"I'll tell you what it is," he said, voice sharp like a blade. "It's the fact that we can say 'ummah' in the masjid but still be segregated by skin tone in every space that matters."

The room froze.

He leaned forward. "You can marry my sister's cooking. You can borrow my slang. But my people? My Blackness? That's still taboo, huh?"

Silence.

"I been Muslim longer than some of y'all been alive. But the second I want to marry someone outside my 'lane,' suddenly I'm not good enough."

His voice cracked.

"I'm tired of it. Tired of pretending it don't hurt. Tired of being told we're 'equal in Islam'—when every wedding, every masjid board, every family dinner says otherwise."

Musa opened his eyes.

Rohan sat up straighter.

Tariq stared at the floor, fists clenched under the chair.

Sonya, seated two rows behind with the sisters, looked directly at Tariq. Their eyes met for a second.

And that second was a fire.

After the event, the air was electric.

Some students left quietly. Others argued in the hallway. Hugs turned to debates. The idealistic flyer now looked like satire.

In the courtyard, under the amber glow of the lampposts, the boys found each other again.

No food. No smiles. Just heat.

"That was... intense," Abe said.

"Needed," Michael added.

Rohan didn't speak.

Tariq did. "You felt that, right?" Everyone looked at him.

"That wasn't just his truth," he said. "That was our truth. All of us. Whether we admit it or not."

Rohan crossed his arms. "It's not that simple."

Tariq turned to him. "What part?"

"The part where we act like it's all racism and nothing else. Culture matters. Family matters."

"And who gets to decide which culture is valid?" Tariq snapped. "Who decides what family deserves respect?"

"Don't make this personal," Rohan warned.

"It is personal," Tariq said, stepping closer. "When I get looked at like I'm less Muslim because I'm not from Karachi or Cairo. When I can't sit next to your cousin without her mom clutching her bag like I'm gonna steal it.

When Sonya—"

He stopped himself. Too late.

Rohan's jaw twitched. "There it is."

Musa stepped in. "Brothers—"

"No," Tariq said, voice tight. "Let him say it."

Rohan looked at him. "You think just because we share space, we share reality? My family came here with trauma, too. Sacrifice, too. Just because my struggle doesn't match yours doesn't make it less real."

"I never said it did."

"But you're saying I'm a racist for honoring where I come from?"

Tariq took a breath. "I'm saying honoring your culture shouldn't mean erasing mine."

Musa looked at both of them. "You are both right. And both wrong."

Abe nodded. "Y'all arguing about fences when we're all in the same cage."

Michael whispered, "And the door's unlocked... but no one wants to leave first."

They stood in that tension. Not broken. But cracked.

Like stained glass—beautiful, sharp, and refracting a light none of them fully understood yet.

Later that night, Tariq couldn't sleep. He opened his journal and wrote:

> *Brotherhood is not peace. It is the promise to return after war.*
> *To sit in silence. To stay in the room when the easy exit is rage.*

The Test of the Circle

No one spoke for two days. Not really. They moved around each other like ghosts—coexisting without colliding.

Tariq spent most of his time in the library, headphones in but no music playing. Rohan typed essays with surgical focus, his face a locked door. Musa stayed out late, praying alone at Masjid Malcolm. Abe floated from lounge to lounge, pretending to be distracted. Hasan buried himself in Econ textbooks and skipped most group meals. Michael simply... watched.

The silence wasn't peaceful. It was avoidance wrapped in politeness. But avoidance is a rot. It grows, slowly and invisibly, until the walls crumble and no one remembers where the foundation was.

It was Tariq who finally cracked.

He walked into the common room after midnight—eyes heavy, throat dry, soul louder than his footsteps. The room was dim, a single desk lamp casting a gold pool across the floor.

Musa sat cross-legged on the rug, finishing his final raka'ah of isha. When he finished, he turned slightly, not surprised to see Tariq standing there.

Tariq didn't wait. "I said things I shouldn't have," he began.

Musa looked up. "You said things that needed saying."

"Still... I lost control."

Musa nodded. "And what did you learn in that loss?"

Tariq sat across from him. "That I want this circle more than I want to be right."

The room stayed still. Then came another voice. "I heard that."

Abe entered from the hallway, hoodie up, socks mismatched, holding a bag of Oreos like it was a sacred offering.

"I'm tired of pretending I'm chill," he said. "I'm not. I'm scared most days. Of failing. Of disappointing people. Of being fake."

Musa smiled softly. "Welcome to the human race."

Then Michael appeared, gently placing his laptop on the floor. "I built an app that logs your prayers," he said. "Not for guilt. Just... for honesty."

Hasan stepped in next. No books. No plans. Just presence.

"I don't know how to say sorry in six languages," he muttered, "but I'm here."

Last came Rohan. He didn't say anything at first. Just sat down.

Tariq looked at him. "We're still good?"

Rohan met his eyes. "Only if we don't pretend we didn't bleed."

Tariq nodded.

Then he pulled the rug toward them. Not for prayer. Just to sit. Together. They formed a circle—imperfect, uneven, sacred.

No one led. No one taught. No one preached.

They just... talked. About what scared them. What shaped them. What haunted them. What they hid behind jokes, silence, sarcasm, and spreadsheets.

They peeled back pride like old wallpaper. They admitted truths they'd never said aloud.

And when they were done, Musa stood. He opened his prayer mat and laid it in the center. Not for obligation. Not because it was time. But because it was right.

The others joined him. No imam. No perfection.

Just sincerity. Just intention. Just faith in motion.

Afterward, they didn't speak. They didn't need to. The silence was no longer distance. It was trust.

That night, before bed, Tariq texted Sonya.

Tariq: "Still figuring things out. But I'm better when I'm around truth. Thanks for seeing me."

She replied an hour later.

Sonya: "Keep building with your brothers. The rest will come."

He smiled, placed the phone screen-down, and looked at the room around him.

Six beds.

Six paths.

One shared fire.

CHAPTER FOUR

The Fire Between Us

When Eyes Begin to Linger

It started with the way Sonya laughed. Not at Tariq's jokes—those were easy, predictable, rehearsed. It was the way she laughed at Abe's sarcasm. At Michael's quiet one-liners. At Rohan's dry, over-articulated business metaphors that weren't even meant to be funny. She laughed like she was in on something. And it made her everybody's favorite.

Even Musa, who rarely engaged with anyone who quoted poets or wore nail polish, would nod when she offered a subtle insight into their MSA study circle. But no one talked about the way Tariq watched her. Not openly. Because they all noticed. And because they were all wondering: what happens when affection isn't private anymore?

A week later, Sonya brought someone new to the table. Her name was Aisha—a second-year pre-pharmacy student with Ghanaian roots, deep dimples, and a laugh that felt like sunshine at dawn. They met her at the MSA's Thursday tea night, hosted in a cramped campus lounge that smelled like cardamom and old carpet. Sonya walked in with Aisha at her side, arms linked like sisters who'd known each other since birth.

"This is the crew," Sonya said. "The Columbia Circle."

Aisha smiled. "The infamous roommates. Heard about y'all already."

Abe grinned. "All good things, right?"

"Depends on who's talking," she said, sipping chai.

They laughed. But Rohan didn't. He just watched her. Like she had just interrupted his rhythm.

Later that night, back at the dorm, the energy was strange. Tariq sat on the windowsill, scrolling through his texts with Sonya, trying not to reread anything too many times. Abe paced with a plastic spoon in his mouth, humming old Tupac under his breath. Hasan had his nose in a finance report, but his fingers kept twitching. Musa was quiet. But not distant. And Rohan? He was somewhere else entirely—staring at a blank page like it owed him an apology.

"You good?" Tariq asked finally.

"Yeah," Rohan said. "Just... distracted."

"By?"

"Nothing important."

But it was. Because by Friday, he was asking Sonya for Aisha's number.

When Aisha agreed to study together, it wasn't dramatic. They met at Butler Library. Shared notes. Talked about pharmacy and marketing. But underneath the textbook banter, something grew.

She was smart. Too smart for fluff. She didn't flirt. But she challenged. She questioned. She asked Rohan why he always spoke like he was presenting a TED Talk. He told her that was how he kept people from getting too close.

She smiled, not in approval—but in recognition.

"You're afraid of soft things," she said.

"No, I'm afraid of weak things."

"They're not the same."

By week's end, Aisha was part of the orbit. She joined them for dinner once. Then again for game night. Then again at Jumu'ah. And suddenly, Sonya wasn't the only gravitational pull in the room.

The brothers noticed. Especially Tariq. And especially when Sonya whispered to Aisha across the table, and Aisha covered her mouth to hide a smile. The kind of smile girls exchange when talking about... possibilities.

That night, Tariq couldn't sleep. He thought about Rohan and Aisha. He thought about Musa watching everyone, silent but observant. He thought about the small, invisible fire that had started in the middle of the group—and how it was growing. Not wild. Not dangerous. But unpredictable.

And all fire, eventually, had to consume something.

He opened his journal.

> *Sonya is a mirror. Aisha is a match. And we are all standing too close to the spark.*

Boundaries and Burning

Tariq didn't plan to tell her that night. He just needed air. He had been sitting in Butler Library for three hours pretending to study case law, but his eyes kept wandering. Not to his phone. Not to the clock. But inward—somewhere murky and loud and increasingly impossible to silence.

So he left. Walked aimlessly through campus until he found himself outside the women's dorms. He didn't even realize he'd texted her until she opened the door, hair wrapped in a scarf, glasses low on her nose, hoodie too big to be hers.

"You good?" she asked.

"Can we walk?"

She didn't hesitate.

They walked toward Riverside Park. No agenda. No laughter. Just silence stretching between them like an invisible rope—tight, trembling, threatening to snap.

Finally, she spoke.

"You're heavy tonight."

He exhaled through his nose. "I'm always heavy. Just better at hiding it."

She waited.

"I think I'm catching feelings," he said, almost too casually.

"For who?"

He smiled, tired. "Don't make me say it."

"You don't have to. I know."

They kept walking.

"So?" she asked, voice soft.

"So it's complicated."

Sonya nodded. "Because of what people will say?"

Tariq shook his head. "Because of what I don't know how to say."

"Then don't say it. Show it."

He stopped walking. She turned to him. And in the streetlamp glow, with the river behind them and the city breathing around them, he said the truth he hadn't dared name until now.

"I want more. With you. But I'm scared of ruining what we already have. I'm scared I'm not enough. That I'm too distracted. Too unsure. That I'm not the guy who gets to love someone like you."

Her eyes didn't waver.

"Do you think you're the only one scared?"

He blinked.

"I built myself from broken pieces, Tariq," she continued. "I carry abandonment in one hand and survival in the other. I don't do casual. I don't do games. So if you're coming... come real."

"I don't know how to be anything else."

She nodded once. "Then we'll see."

She didn't hug him. Didn't kiss him. She just took his hand—for a moment. And then let go. Because real things don't rush. They rise.

Back at the dorm, Rohan was facing something harder than feelings. He was on the phone with his father. The conversation had started with business numbers—exports, weather conditions, mango yields. Then, a sharp pivot.

"I hear you've been spending time with a girl."

Rohan's stomach turned. "Who told you that?"

"It doesn't matter. Is it true?"

"She's... in my friend circle. We study together."

"Is she Pakistani?"

"No."

"Is she Muslim?"

"Yes."

"Does she speak Urdu?"

"No."

"Then she is not for you."

Rohan gripped the edge of his desk.

"Appa... I'm not proposing. I'm just getting to know her."

"That's how it starts. And then you shame us. You disgrace your mother. You throw away a thousand years of family for... for an outsider."

"She's not an outsider."

"She's not us."

The call ended soon after. No goodbye. Just static. Rohan sat there, the words echoing like a slap. *She's not us.* But she felt more real than any "us" he had ever known.

The next day, Aisha showed up at the library with her usual smile. Rohan was already there, waiting with coffee. She sat, opened her notebook, and looked at him.

"You okay?"

He hesitated. Then: "Can I ask you something dangerous?"

"Only if you ask it slow."

He looked her in the eyes.

"What would you do if someone told you you weren't enough because of where you're from?"

She didn't flinch.

"I'd pray for them. Then live in a way that made them regret ever opening their mouth."

He smiled, but it didn't reach his eyes.

"Then I guess I've got work to do."

That night, the brothers gathered for a group dinner. Not formal. Not planned. Just instinct. But the energy was off. Abe kept cracking jokes no one laughed at. Hasan scrolled aimlessly. Michael brought two laptops but didn't open either. Musa said the bare minimum. And Tariq? He was trying to stay present. But his thoughts were still by the river. With her.

Rohan sat directly across from him. Their eyes met once. It was brief. But something passed between them—acknowledgment, envy, understanding, resentment. None of it spoken. All of it real.

Later, in his journal, Tariq wrote:

> *Fire doesn't destroy everything. Sometimes it clears the path. Burns the brush. Exposes what we were too scared to see. But the thing about fire is… Once it starts, you can't choose where it spreads*

Collateral Sparks

The storm broke on a Sunday afternoon. It wasn't loud at first. No shouting. No slamming doors. Just tension—thick and hot—simmering beneath the surface of every conversation, every sidelong glance, every carefully chosen silence.

It started when Sonya came over. Not for Tariq. Not for drama. Just to drop off Aisha's notebook. She stepped into the dorm like she always had—familiar, fearless, the only woman they let pass their threshold without awkwardness. Except today… the awkwardness was waiting.

Musa stood near the bookshelf, arms crossed, eyes steady.

"Is Aisha not with you?" he asked.

"She's in lab," Sonya replied. "I just came to—"

"You shouldn't be here."

The air shifted.

Tariq stood from his desk. "Bro—"

Musa raised a hand. "I'm speaking."

Sonya tilted her head. "I've been here before."

"Then maybe we've been too lenient before."

Tariq stepped forward. "You're out of line."

Musa looked at him. "And you've lost yours."

Silence.

Sonya blinked slowly. "Say what you mean, Musa."

"I mean this space was supposed to be a sanctuary," he said. "A place for brothers to sharpen each other, to hold each other accountable, to grow."

"And I've interrupted that?"

"You've... complicated it."

She laughed once. Not from humor. From disbelief.

"So I'm a distraction now?"

No one answered. She looked at Tariq.

He didn't speak.

And that silence? That was the sharpest blade in the room.

Later, after she left, the conversation cracked open like a wound. Musa didn't raise his voice. He didn't need to.

"I watched all of you shift," he said. "Change your habits. Skip prayers. Skip check-ins. All for... charm."

"It's not just about her," Abe said.

"But she was the match," Musa replied. "And we all brought our own dry grass."

Hasan leaned forward. "So what—you want to ban women from our lives? Pretend we're monks?"

"I want us to be honest," Musa said. "If we are building something holy, we have to protect its foundation."

Tariq's jaw was tight. His voice low. "So who gets to decide what's holy? You?"

"I decide for myself," Musa said. "But we said this was a brotherhood. And lately... it feels like a stage."

Michael nodded slowly. "The algorithm's broken. Too many inputs. Not enough clarity."

Abe frowned. "Yo, speak human."

Michael looked up. "Everyone's making moves based on fear and fire. And none of us are talking about it. So the code's messy. The results? Chaotic."

Rohan folded his arms. "So what? We cut her off? Stop liking people? Suppress who we are?"

Musa shook his head. "We remember who we said we wanted to become. And we act accordingly."

The room fell quiet. Not because they disagreed. But because they did. Because part of them wanted to be righteous. And part of them just wanted to be free.

Meanwhile, Sonya sat on a bench near the journalism building, fingers wrapped around a coffee cup she hadn't sipped in twenty minutes. Aisha sat beside her.

"He finally said it," Sonya murmured.

Aisha knew what she meant.

"That you don't belong?"

Sonya nodded. "Not in those words. But in that... tone. That posture."

"You okay?"

Sonya smiled, but it didn't reach her eyes.

"I always knew this was borrowed space. Even when they laughed at my jokes. Even when they asked for my notes. Even when they said I was different."

Aisha said nothing. Because she knew that feeling too. The slow realization that even admiration has borders. That even love has rules. That in some spaces, your warmth is welcome. But your weight? Your full, unruly, feminine, powerful self? That's a threat.

That night, Musa prayed alone. Again. But something in the prayer felt different. Not colder. Just quieter. He didn't feel right. But he didn't feel wrong either. Just... unsure.

He finished, folded his prayer mat, and looked around the room. They were all there. But they weren't together. Not like before. Not yet.

In his journal, Tariq wrote:

> *I wanted fire. I wanted clarity. I wanted truth that moved like water over stone. Instead, I got silence that feels like judgment. And eyes that look like doors slowly closing. If this is what it takes to be righteous—Why does it feel like exile?*

What Fire Leaves Behind

Sonya didn't come around for a week. No texts. No Thursday tea nights. No MSA events. Even her online presence dimmed—no Instagram stories, no replies to group chats.

Tariq noticed every absence like a skipped heartbeat. He typed messages and deleted them. Rewrote entire paragraphs in his Notes app before scrapping them again. The silence didn't feel like anger. It felt like... retreat. He told himself it was temporary. He told himself she just needed space. But deep down, a quieter voice whispered: "You didn't protect her. Not from Musa. Not from the expectations. Not from the ache of realizing she was welcome only if she stayed small enough to not disturb the structure."

In the dorm, things moved on. But nothing moved the same. Hasan filled the silence with finance lectures and random debates. Abe kept bouncing between being the comic relief and the spiritual guilt sponge. Michael doubled down on coding, rarely making eye contact, but always listening. Musa... remained Musa. Punctual. Calm. Withdrawn.

And Rohan? He stopped showing up. At first, it was just skipped meals. Then skipped prayers. Then full days away—no word, no explanation. When he did return, he looked... lighter. But distant.

"Everything cool?" Tariq asked one night.

Rohan shrugged. "Depends who you ask."

"You good with Aisha?"

"She's good," he said. "But I think I'm not the guy she thought I could be."

Tariq studied him. "What does that mean?"

Rohan looked away. "It means I told her the truth. About my parents. About what they'd never accept. About what I couldn't promise."

Tariq exhaled. "She say anything back?"

"She said she'd pray for my courage. Then she walked away."

He said it without bitterness. Almost with relief.

"Maybe that's what love is," Rohan added. "Letting go before it ruins you."

Tariq nodded. "Or maybe it's standing in the ruin and choosing to rebuild."

They both sat with that. Neither claiming to know which was true.

That Friday, Musa led prayer in their dorm again. No announcement. Just presence. He laid the mat down. Started with dhikr. Recited slowly. With weight.

They all joined. Not for performance. Not for guilt. But for stillness. Even Rohan. Even Tariq. No Sonya. No Aisha. Just the six of them. Knees touching. Breath syncing. Souls quieting.

And when the final salam was given, no one rushed to move. They just sat. Together. In what fire had left behind: Ash. Clarity. And the beginning of something rebuilt. Not perfect. Not painless. But real.

That night, Tariq walked alone to Riverside Park. The spot where she once held his hand. He pulled out his phone and finally sent the message.

Tariq: "I'm sorry I let the room shrink when I should've made it bigger. You deserved more space. You still do."

The message stayed unread for hours. Until just after midnight.

Sonya: "Thank you. I needed that. I'm rooting for all of you. From a little farther away now."

He stared at the words for a long time. Then placed the phone face down. Closed his eyes. And whispered a du'a for her peace. For their growth. And for the fire inside him to stop devouring, and start illuminating.

CHAPTER FIVE

Thresholds

Distance Measured in Silence

Time didn't explode this time. It drifted.

Three weeks passed like fog—thick, invisible, but strangely heavy. The campus changed colors as October crept in. Hoodies replaced T-shirts. Conversations moved indoors. The first midterms came and went like warnings.

The brotherhood didn't break. But it bent. Not all at once. Just in increments.

Musa still led prayer—twice a week now, instead of every day. He no longer corrected their missed raka'ahs or half-whispered surahs. He just prayed. And left the mat open.

Rohan returned to group meals. But not as himself. He smiled, contributed, said all the right things—but his gaze was always slightly elsewhere. Focused inward. Focused far.

Michael started sleeping less. Coding more. Once, he stayed up three straight nights rebuilding a web plugin that no one had asked for.

Hasan locked into a Wall Street internship path. His Google Calendar began to look like the periodic table. Fifteen-minute increments of productivity. Even his du'a time was color-coded.

Abe started ghosting. Sometimes he was the loudest in the room. Sometimes he disappeared for days, claiming study groups, late night prayers, "mental resets." But no one really knew where he went.

And Tariq? Tariq stopped writing. The journal stayed closed. He still showed up to everything. Still listened. Still made everyone laugh when the silence got too loud. But inside, something had gone quiet. Not broken. Just... withdrawn.

One Wednesday night, after everyone else had gone to sleep, he found himself walking again. Riverside. Always Riverside. The water didn't talk back. It just moved. Like him.

He pulled out his phone. No unread messages. No notifications. Sonya had gone radio silent. Not out of malice. Out of maturity. And that made it harder. Because there was no villain to blame. Just time. And the things it slowly erases.

Back at the dorm, Musa sat alone in the common room, holding a letter in his lap. It was from home. Handwritten. Torn at the corners.

His youngest brother had sent it with a drawing enclosed—a stick figure in a kufi holding a Qur'an in one hand and a money bag in the other. Underneath, it said: "My hero."

Musa's throat tightened. He hadn't sent money in a month. The last deposit had gone to tuition.

He prayed harder. Longer. But the guilt didn't go away. So he started fasting again. Not for the reward. For the clarity.

The next morning, the group crossed paths on their way to class. No arguments. No drama. Just passing.

Hasan offered Tariq a nod.

Abe slapped his shoulder with a joke that didn't land.

Rohan muttered something about office hours.

Michael gave a tired smile.

Musa walked with a Qur'an translation tucked under his arm.

Tariq watched them all walk away. Each one pulling in a different direction.

And he wondered—*Is this how brotherhood dies? Not with war. But with drift.*

That night, he sat on the floor of his room and opened the journal again. For the first time in weeks. And he wrote:

> *There is no loud betrayal here. No blood on the rug. Just friendship growing thin/ Like a rope pulled by silence and success. We are still brothers. We just forgot how to say it. When the lights are off.*

The Scholars and the Shadows

Professor Akhtar's classroom didn't look like much.

Dim lighting. Worn carpet. Walls lined with dry-erase boards half-smeared from past lectures. The only thing remarkable about the room was how ordinary it felt—until the man himself entered.

He was older—gray-bearded, low-voiced, and deceptively casual. His dress code rarely changed: navy blue sweaters, khakis, scuffed oxfords, a watch that never left his wrist.

But when he spoke, the room bent.

Today's topic: *"Justice, or Just Us?"*

Tariq had heard of him through campus buzz—*"The Radical,"* they called him. The professor who brought Malcolm into legal theory and made students cry during office hours without ever raising his voice.

Tariq wasn't enrolled in the class. He had just wandered in.

He sat in the back. Hoodie on. No notes. Just ears. And listened.

"There's no such thing as neutral law," Akhtar said, pacing slowly. "Only law written by the victorious and enforced against the vulnerable."

A few students nodded. Others frowned.

Akhtar continued. "You want to be a lawyer? A judge? A politician?

Fine. But don't call yourself a servant of justice if you've never knelt beside the people crushed by the systems you want to control."

Tariq sat up straighter.

"You've read case law. Great. But have you sat in a courtroom where the defendant has a public defender with forty-nine active cases and three kids at home? Have you seen a mother beg for a plea deal that will still rip her from her child's life because 'it's the best we can get'?"

The room went still.

Then Akhtar looked up, eyes scanning every face.

"And don't tell me about activism if you can't tell me where the nearest housing court is."

After class, Tariq stayed behind. He didn't know why. Something in him felt pulled.

Akhtar noticed. "You're not on the roster."

"No, sir. I just... sat in."

The professor nodded. "What's your name?"

"Tariq."

"And what are you studying, Tariq?"

"Pre-law."

Akhtar raised an eyebrow. "That's a major now?"

Tariq smirked. "Technically political science. With an eye toward law school."

"Whose law?"

Tariq blinked. "Excuse me?"

Akhtar repeated, slower this time. "Whose law are you pursuing? Who does it serve? Who does it ignore?"

Tariq swallowed. "I'm... still figuring that out."

Akhtar nodded once. "Good. When you're ready to stop studying law and start studying power—my door's open."

Meanwhile, Abe was unraveling. Not publicly.

He still made people laugh. Still flirted with the girls in the business program. Still dressed like streetwear royalty. But when he got home that night, he locked himself in the dorm bathroom. Turned on the faucet. Sat on the closed toilet lid. And just... breathed.

He had received another voicemail from his father that morning.

Another reminder.

Another accusation.

"You're wasting our name. You're playing games in that city. I didn't pay for you to become a poor man's preacher."

Abe had deleted the voicemail without replying. But it echoed all day.

So he came home. Locked the door. Sat on the cold tile. And cried.

Not loudly. Not dramatically. Just... finally.

Tariq found him there, forty minutes later. He knocked gently.

"You good?"

Abe didn't answer at first. Then, "Give me five."

Tariq paused. "I'll be out here."

Fifteen minutes passed before the door creaked open. Abe's eyes were red, but his face was clean. Calm.

Tariq didn't ask questions. He just handed him a bottle of water and sat down beside him.

On the floor. Back against the wall. Like they used to during orientation week when the world was wide and their brotherhood felt unshakable.

"I think I'm done pretending I don't care," Abe finally said.

Tariq nodded. "About what?"

"About being good. About being... enough. For them. For God. For me."

"You are."

Abe laughed bitterly. "I don't even know what 'good' looks like anymore. Musa prays perfect. Michael's basically a monk. Rohan's halfway to being a sheikh-slash-CEO. And you? You walk around like you're trying to save the world."

Tariq shook his head. "Nah, bro. I'm just trying to survive it."

Silence.

Then Abe asked: "When do we stop faking it?"

Tariq answered without looking up. "When we trust each other enough to not have to."

Back in his room, Tariq opened his laptop and emailed Professor Akhtar.

Subject line: Learning to Unlearn

Professor—

I want in. Not just the class. The work. The truth. I'm tired of reciting dreams that don't belong to me. Teach me how to break the mold.

Respectfully,

—Tariq R.

He hit send.

And something cracked open inside.

Fractures in the Frame

Hasan's spreadsheet had thirty-two color-coded tabs. One for each course. One for prayer schedules. One for internship applications. One for networking contacts. A tab for Arabic vocabulary drills. A tab for gym reps. Even a tab for "du'a intensity," which he scored daily on a scale from 1 to 10.

He tracked everything. Except how tired he was.

The exhaustion crept in like fog—quiet and dignified. He didn't miss deadlines. He didn't break down. But somewhere between Fajr and LinkedIn notifications, his mind stopped resting.

He forgot to eat twice in one week. Missed two prayers. Skipped three hangouts. By the fourth, no one even asked.

It was 3:11 a.m. when he collapsed. Not physically. Emotionally.

He was at the library, surrounded by law students twice his age, prepping a pitch deck for an internship he wasn't even sure he wanted anymore.

He blinked at his screen. Eyes blurry. Hands shaking.

And then... nothing. Not sleep. Not panic. Just numbness.

He walked out. Phone off. Backpack half-zipped. He didn't even remember how he got back to the dorm.

When he opened the door, Michael was still awake—coding in the dark, glasses low on his nose, screen bathing him in soft blue light.

Hasan stood there for a moment.

Michael didn't look up. "You good?"

Hasan didn't answer. Just dropped his bag. Sat down on the floor. And whispered, "I can't breathe in my own schedule anymore."

Michael finally turned. They sat like that for a while—one on the floor, the other still wrapped in blue light.

"You ever feel like your whole life is a group project you didn't ask for?" Hasan muttered.

Michael closed his laptop slowly. "Every day."

"You're so calm, though."

"That's not calm," Michael said. "That's control."

He looked down. "I haven't talked to my mother in three weeks. Haven't called home. Haven't told anyone I'm fasting on random weekdays just so I have an excuse not to join anyone for dinner."

Hasan turned. "Why?"

"Because if I eat alone, no one sees how lonely I really am."

Hasan stared at him. "I didn't know."

"You weren't supposed to."

"Why not?"

Michael paused. Then: "Because I built my identity around being the guy who doesn't need anything. And now... I don't know how to ask."

They sat in that silence. Not as strangers. Not even just as friends. But as two young men realizing that brilliance, discipline, and faith didn't save you from loneliness—they just hid it better.

The next morning, Michael broke routine. He skipped his 7 a.m. solo coding block. And joined the group for breakfast. First time in weeks.

Abe blinked. "Whoa. Our tech prophet has descended from the cloud."

Michael cracked a soft smile. "Y'all make bad coffee."

Laughter. Real laughter. The kind they hadn't heard in days.

Even Musa smiled. Even Hasan.

Later that day, Hasan deleted two tabs from his spreadsheet. No announcement. No speech. Just... delete.

He added a new one: "Unmeasurable Things." Under it, he wrote:

Eye contact with someone who sees me
Sitting still without shame
Laughing without planning it
Making du'a without ranking it
Friendship that doesn't need apology
Presence that doesn't require performance

And then, for the first time in weeks—He closed the laptop. And went for a walk. Without a destination.

That evening, the dorm was quiet but alive. No deep talks. No philosophical showdowns. Just presence.

Michael shared a coding trick with Abe, who pretended to understand. Musa made extra tea and poured it for everyone without asking. Hasan sat on the floor instead of his desk chair. Tariq read a poem aloud from a book he'd found in the laundry room. Even Rohan wandered in and asked, "Y'all got leftovers?"

The brotherhood hadn't healed. Not fully. But something real had returned.

The ability to show up. Even when you're unsure. Even when you're unraveling. Even when the future feels like a fog you can't code or spreadsheet your way through.

That night, Michael updated his personal GitHub profile.

He added a new repository: "HumanOS: A Social Survival Code." The description read, "A messy, untested, emotionally overloaded system architecture for surviving faith, friendship, and New York at 19 years old. Under "Status," he wrote: "In Development. Permanently."

The Return of Intention

It started with a text. Sent by Musa at 8:04 p.m. No emojis. No hashtags. No voice notes. Just: "Halaqah. Our room. 9PM. Come as you are."

That last line hit different.

Come as you are. Not "bring Qur'an." Not "make wudu." Just—show up.

Tariq was the first to reply. "Bet."

Then Michael. "On my way."

Then Abe. Then Hasan.

Rohan said nothing. But he came.

By 9:07, all six of them were seated on the floor—cross-legged, mismatched socks, some with hoodies still on, others wrapped in blankets.

No shoes. No expectations. No rank.

Musa sat at the head of the circle, not because he wanted to—but because they still looked to him when the room needed stillness.

He cleared his throat. Spoke without pretense.

"No lecture tonight," he began. "No hadith marathon. I just want us to talk."

They waited.

He looked around the circle. "What are you holding right now? Don't lie. Don't edit. Don't impress. Just say it."

They hesitated.

Then Tariq spoke. "I'm holding doubt. In myself. In what I'm studying. In whether I'm really who I say I am."

Musa nodded. "Next."

Hasan shifted. "I'm holding exhaustion. I thought if I built a system strong enough, it would carry me. But I'm still the one dragging it."

Michael added, "I'm holding silence. I've been alone so long I forgot how to let people care about me."

Abe rubbed his hands together. "I'm holding guilt. For frontin' so much, I don't even know who I'd be if I dropped the act."

Then came Rohan. He looked down. Then up.

"I'm holding grief. For a version of me I wanted to become. For a love I couldn't honor. For the cost of tradition."

They all turned to Musa.

He breathed in, then out. "I'm holding fear. That all this faith I've studied—memorized—won't save me from pride. That I'll lose the softness I need to lead."

Silence. Not heavy. Not shameful. Just... honest.

Tariq looked around. "This," he said. "This is what I came to college for."

Michael nodded. "Same."

Musa reached into his desk and pulled out a small speaker. Pressed play.

The voice of Qur'an filled the room—Surah Ash-Sharh. 'Have We not expanded your chest?'

The sound washed over them. Verse by verse. Not sermon. Not warning. Just a balm.

They listened. Some with tears. Some with stillness. Some with hope rising like breath after a long plunge.

When the recitation ended, no one moved.

Tariq broke the silence. "Can we do this weekly?"

"Or more," Hasan added.

Abe grinned. "Next time, I'll bring snacks."

Michael smiled. "Spiritual snacks or...?"

"Both," Musa said, laughing for the first time in days.

Even Rohan cracked a grin.

As they stood to pray together, it wasn't formal. No rows. No announcements.

Just brothers standing side by side. Facing east. Facing truth.

That night, back in his bed, Tariq wrote one line in his journal:

> *We are not perfect. But we are present. And that—maybe— is enough.*

CHAPTER SIX

Broken Mirrors, New Names

Names We Didn't Choose

Mid-October brought more than a drop in temperature. It brought midterms, internships, internal ruptures, and something no one in the group had expected: labels. Heavy ones. Quietly assigned. Passed around classrooms and group chats like unspoken name tags no one had asked for.

Tariq found out during his public policy seminar. He was answering a question—something about redlining and housing inequality—when a girl in the second row whispered just loud enough for him to hear: "That's the Black Muslim activist guy, right?"

She didn't mean harm. She probably thought it was a compliment.

But it landed like a sentence.

Tariq paused. Lost his train of thought. He finished the comment. Sat down. Felt his face flush.

He wasn't mad. Not exactly. But something tightened in his chest.

He was now a "type." Not a thinker. Not a student. Not a complex human navigating contradiction. Just: The Black Muslim activist guy.

Later that week, Rohan got a different name.

It came during a networking mixer for South Asian business students. He wore his best blazer. Ironed his shirt. Smiled at all the right people. Told all the right stories.

But when he casually mentioned working on a marketing project with Aisha—"just as friends," he added—one of the seniors pulled him aside.

"You know your parents won't go for that, right?"

Rohan blinked. "Go for what?"

"Come on, bro. Don't play dumb. Ghanaian? Pre-med? You're a Siddiqui. You know how this works."

Rohan smiled politely. Nodded. Laughed it off.

But later that night, he stared at himself in the dorm mirror for twenty full minutes. Whispered the word "Siddiqui" under his breath. Not like a name. Like a shackle.

In the group, other names floated quietly: Michael was "the quiet genius."

Musa was "the sheikh."

Abe was "the joker."

Hasan was "the finance guy."

Tariq was "the activist."

Rohan was "the diplomat."

None of them had chosen these. But the world had. And now they were expected to wear them like second skins. Even when they didn't fit. Even when they itched.

It was during this quiet identity crisis that Sonya resurfaced. Not with a text. Not with a visit. With a post. A short-form essay shared on the Columbia MSA's blog, written under her full name: Sonya Liyana Ramos.

Tariq saw it first. The title: "When Community Means Conditional"

The post was gentle, poetic, devastating.

It spoke of women who get invited into Muslim spaces until they take up too much room. Of girls who quote Rumi and Audre Lorde, and are told to "be more modest." Of girls who wear hijab one day and wrap their hair the next and are told, "Sister, you're confusing us." Of love interests turned into liabilities. Of spiritual homes that only open their doors halfway.

> *I was never told I didn't belong. But I was never made to feel like I fully did. Somewhere in between invisibility and hyper-visibility is where many of us live. And we build family there, even when no one calls it home.*

Tariq read it three times. By the fourth, he had to close his laptop. He didn't cry. But he felt something burn in his chest. He had wanted her to stay. But he'd never fought for her right to be.

Abe found the post an hour later. He didn't say anything to anyone.

But he did close his bedroom door and stand in front of the mirror. Not flexing. Not posturing. Just looking. At his face. His name. His silence. His complicity.

And he whispered: "I'm sorry."

Rohan read it, too. He sent no reaction.

But he opened his Notes app that night and wrote:

> *The women we fail to protect are the women who teach us what we were too scared to become.*

He never showed it to anyone.

In their own ways, they were all confronting the same truth. They had names they didn't choose. Scripts they didn't write. And they were tired. Not of the world calling them those things. But of how easily they'd accepted the roles. How hard they had worked to earn them.

The next night, Tariq went to Akhtar's office hours. Not for law. For clarity.

He sat across from the professor, hands folded, voice uncertain. "I don't think I want to be a lawyer anymore."

Akhtar nodded once. "Then stop preparing for a future you don't believe in."

Tariq swallowed. "What if I disappoint people?"

"You will," Akhtar said calmly. "That's how you know you're telling the truth."

That same hour, Musa found himself sitting on the floor of the masjid library. Not reading. Just staring at the shelves of books, all with names on the spines.

Men who had died centuries ago. Men who had once been boys. Lost, messy, unsure.

He whispered their names. Then whispered his own. And wondered which parts of it were real.

That night, for the first time in months, Tariq pulled out his Qur'an. Not out of obligation. Out of longing.

He didn't read for memorization. He read for reminder. And found this:

Indeed, We have created you from male and female and made you peoples and tribes so that you may know one another. (Surah Al-Hujurat, 49:13)

Know one another. Not judge. Not label. Know.

He closed the book. Closed his eyes. And whispered into the dark: "I'm ready to meet the version of me I haven't met yet."

The Cost of Becoming

Tariq stood in the middle of Hamilton Hall, gripping the withdrawal form with both hands like it might explode. He'd already written the reason on the dotted line: "Change in academic direction." But that was a lie.

The real reason? I don't believe in this anymore. Not the track. Not the titles. Not the clean path from Columbia to courtrooms. Not the idea that justice comes from bar exams and firm letters and a nameplate on a polished door.

He had walked into Akhtar's class again that morning. Just sat in the back, no notebook, no questions. Just eyes wide and soul open. The professor lectured on Frederick Douglass and Angela Davis, on justice by interruption and truth as confrontation. At the end of class, he said something that hit like a bat to the ribs: "The people you most want to impress are often the ones least equipped to hold your truth."

Tariq didn't need a follow-up email. Or a second opinion. He just walked straight to the registrar's office. And stood there. Form in hand. Breath shallow. For twenty minutes. Then, slowly—he folded the form and put it in his pocket. Not out of fear. But because he needed to talk to his people first. Really talk.

Across campus, Rohan was pacing outside Dodge Hall with his phone pressed so tight to his ear it left a mark. His father's voice was calm. Which made it worse.

"You have one semester," he said. "Then you return. MBA begins immediately. Family business is not a negotiation."

"Appa, I haven't even—"

"You're not an artist, Rohan. You're not a philosopher. You're not a revolutionary. You are Siddiqui. You inherit. You execute. You do not wander."

"I'm not wandering."

"You are stalling."

There was a pause. Then his father added: "And stop talking to girls who don't understand the weight of your name." The line went dead.

Rohan stood there, fists trembling, breath quick. People walked past him, headphones in, backpacks slung, laughing. No one saw the fracture happen. But it split straight through his core. He sat down on the stone bench beside the hall, staring at the ground. For a long time.

Meanwhile, Musa opened a letter from home. Paper. Ink. Folded carefully, but with urgency in the creases. From his older sister. The only one who still wrote.

The well is dry again. Mama is sick more often than not. We are proud of you. But the village is watching. They say, "Where is the help he promised?" I told them you are studying. They say: "Studying doesn't fill our bellies."

He read it twice. Then placed it gently on his prayer mat. He sat cross-legged. Stared at the wall. And whispered, "Ya Allah... am I failing them? Or are they asking for what I cannot give?"

He didn't cry. He didn't collapse. But that night, when the group gathered to eat, he barely touched his food. And no one asked why.

At 8:45 p.m., Tariq walked into the study lounge on the third floor of Lerner Hall. He wasn't there to study. He wasn't even sure why he came. Until he saw her.

Sonya. In the corner. Hoodie up. Glasses sliding. Laptop open. He paused.

She didn't look up. Not right away.

But after a few seconds, she closed her laptop and turned toward him.

"You saw the post?"

He nodded.

"I meant every word," she said.

"I know," he replied.

Silence. Not awkward. Not empty. Just full.

Finally, she said, "So what now?"

"I think I'm about to disappoint a lot of people."

"Welcome to the club."

Tariq laughed softly.

"You doing okay?"

"I'm writing," she said.

"That's how I stay sane."

"You think we'll ever be what we were before?"

She looked him in the eyes. "I don't want what we were. I want what we can be."

Tariq nodded. "I might drop law."

She blinked. "That's not small."

"It feels right. But... scary."

Sonya smiled. "Anything worth becoming will cost you the comfort of who you were pretending to be."

She didn't say more. She didn't need to.

That night, Tariq called a meeting. In their dorm. No food. No agenda. Just: "Come through. I need to speak."

They showed up. Every one of them. Even Rohan. Even Musa.

Tariq stood at the center of the room. "I've been thinking," he began, "about names." They listened.

"I've been chasing something that never felt like mine. Law. Prestige. Safe success. But every step felt like walking deeper into a costume."

He paused.

"I'm not that guy. I don't want to be a courtroom warrior in a suit with polished shoes and dead eyes."

Abe whistled low. "Say it louder."

Tariq continued. "I want to work with people. With kids. With folks who aren't heard. I want to study social work. And I don't care if it makes me broke or boring or disappointing."

No one laughed. No one clapped. But everyone felt it.

Then Rohan stood. "I'm supposed to inherit a mango empire," he said flatly. "But I want to build something new. For me. Not for a name. Not for a lineage. Just... mine."

He didn't elaborate. He didn't have to.

Hasan, usually silent during moments like these, said: "Let's write new names for ourselves."

Michael whispered, "Ones we choose this time."

Musa didn't speak. He just nodded. Slowly. Deliberately. Then whispered, "Bismillah."

Revolutions and Reverberations

Musa opened the WhatsApp message with shaking hands. It was a voice note. Four minutes long. From his uncle back home in Gambia.

He almost didn't press play. Almost deleted it. But his finger hovered. And then tapped.

The message played in Wolof, the cadence sharp and sorrowful. Musa translated it in real time, each sentence a stone in his gut.

> *The roof is leaking again. Mama is sleeping in her scarf to stay warm. The neighbors talk. They say the boy we raised with Qur'an has forgotten us.*
>
> *You wear their clothes, speak their tongue. But where is your heart, Musa? Is it still here, or have you traded it for their lights and towers?*
>
> *They said you were Hafiz. But a Hafiz feeds the people. A Hafiz builds wells. A Hafiz does not forget.*
>
> *If you come back with only your degrees, we will build you no feast. We will ask: "Where is the barakah?"*

Musa didn't cry. He didn't break the phone. He simply placed it face down and sat on his prayer rug. And for the first time since arriving in America, he asked himself: *What if I'm not the man they believe I am? And what if I never was?*

Rohan's fallout came by email. A brief, formal note from his father's personal assistant:

> *Your father is suspending all wire transfers effective immediately. He requests proof of academic alignment with agreed goals. Any deviation will result in the full withdrawal of financial support.*

Beneath that, in bold:

No discussion.

Rohan closed the email. Then shut his laptop. Then sat perfectly still in the dark.

He thought of mango trees. Of the land his grandfather had walked barefoot to water. Of his name, stitched into generations.

And then he thought of Aisha. Of the way her voice softened when she spoke of medicine. Of the way her laugh made logic irrelevant.

And he whispered, "Maybe being cut off is how freedom begins."

At Columbia's Academic Advising Office, Tariq sat in a small, cold room across from a white woman in a pink cardigan and thick glasses.

"So, social work," she said, clicking her pen.

He nodded.

"You know that's a pivot."

"I do."

"And you're okay with that?"

"No," he said. "But I'm ready for it."

She looked up. Something in his voice must've landed. She adjusted her glasses.

"Not many students come in with this level of clarity."

"I don't have clarity," he replied. "I have conviction."

She smiled.

"That'll do."

They filed the paperwork. And just like that, the path changed.

Friday afternoon, the brothers met again. All six. This time, in the courtyard outside Low Library.

The air was crisp. Autumn's sharpness biting through their sweatshirts and pride.

Sonya was there, too. She hadn't asked. Tariq hadn't invited. She just... showed up. A quiet nod to their unspoken agreement: *I'll come back if you make space.*

The group circled up like always. Loose. Undisciplined. Familiar.

Abe brought chips. Michael brought silence. Hasan had a legal pad with nothing written on it. Rohan wore an old sweater instead of a blazer. Musa came last. His eyes were darker than usual.

They sat. Talked. But not about classes.

They talked about becoming. About what happens when the names you were given no longer fit. When the path you're walking splinters in two.

Sonya listened mostly.

Until Tariq asked: "You ever want to just disappear and come back as your truest self?"

She sipped her tea.

"You don't need to disappear. You need to *unlearn who you had to be just to survive.*"

Musa stirred. "That's dangerous. Unlearning too much."

"Maybe," she said. "But staying hidden is dangerous too."

The words sat heavy.

Rohan said, "My father thinks I'm lost."

Abe muttered, "My father thinks I'm fake."

Musa whispered, "My people think I'm gone."

Tariq looked around the circle. "And what do we think we are?"

Michael finally spoke. "In progress."

That night, Musa didn't sleep. He prayed. Longer than usual. Not to ask for more. But to ask for mercy. To ask for peace.

He wrote in his notebook:

> *I am not the savior. I am not the sacrifice. I am just a son trying not to drown in the expectation of becoming a prophet. Ya Allah, let me be honest with them— and still be loved.*

Sonya texted Tariq that night.

Sonya: "Thank you for making space today."

Tariq: "Thank you for taking it. That mattered."

Sonya: "It's starting to feel like we're all becoming something. Even if we don't know what yet."

Tariq: "As long as we're becoming together."

She didn't reply right away. When she did, it simply said: "Then don't stop walking."

Naming the Pain

It began with a question.

They were gathered again in the dorm—this time by intention. No snacks. No side convos. No chill. Just chairs pulled into a circle, knees close enough to knock, hearts close enough to hear.

Musa had agreed to let Sonya join Not easily. Not confidently. But openly.

Tariq had asked: "Can we be honest?"

Musa had responded: "Only if it's for growth. Not for spectacle."

And Sonya? She showed up early. Hoodie. Headwrap. No makeup. No armor. Just truth.

The first half hour was quiet. Small talk. Nervous laughter.

Then Abe said it. Just... said it. "I hate praying sometimes."

No one responded. So he continued. "I hate it because I feel fake. I stand there and say words I don't fully understand, thinking about things I'm not proud of. I try to clean myself up, but it's like... I don't know who I'm trying to impress anymore."

Musa sat up straighter. But he didn't interrupt.

Abe looked down. "My pops thinks I'm religious now. Because I post Qur'an quotes and show up for Eid. But I haven't read Qur'an in a month. And some nights I drink. Some nights I text girls I shouldn't. Some mornings I don't pray because I feel too dirty to even try."

Silence. Raw. Unfiltered.

Tariq exhaled. "You're not alone."

Abe's eyes lifted. "Then why does it feel like I am?"

Michael said, "Because shame's a shape that fits each of us differently. But we all wear it."

Hasan spoke next. But not with his usual polish. He leaned forward, elbows on knees.

"I've built my whole life around control. Plans. Productivity. Praise. I thought if I stayed two steps ahead of failure, I'd never feel it. But I'm tired, bro."

He swallowed. "My schedule makes room for everything but joy. Everything but softness. Everything but rest. I haven't hugged my little sister in two years because I'm too busy being impressive."

No one clapped. But every heart in the room bowed in recognition.

Then Sonya cleared her throat. Soft. But sharp. "I've been silent long enough."

Musa looked up. Their eyes met. She didn't flinch.

"You say this space is sacred. That this brotherhood is built on faith. But what do you do when your faith makes women feel small?"

Musa blinked. Sonya continued.

"You didn't say it outright. You didn't curse me or call me names. But you didn't protect me, either. You didn't make room for my full presence. You tolerated me until I got too loud. Too visible. Too complicated."

Abe shifted.

Hasan rubbed the back of his neck.

Michael looked at the floor.

Musa didn't move.

Sonya's voice didn't tremble. "You call that accountability. I call it control."

Then she looked at the others. "All of you say you want to be real. But you stay silent when it's not your wound. You nod when it's safe. You speak up when it costs you nothing."

Tariq opened his mouth.

She held up a hand. "Let me finish."

He nodded. Sat back.

She turned back to Musa. "I'm not your enemy. But I'm not your ornament, either. I'm not your sister only when I'm silent. I'm your sister when I disrupt you. When I challenge you. When I ask for a seat and bring my full voice to it."

The room held its breath.

Then—Musa nodded. Once. Slowly. "I hear you."

She waited.

He added: "And I'm sorry. For every time I made you shrink to fit my idea of sanctity. I confused presence with purity. I confused humility with invisibility. I see you now."

Sonya blinked. And for the first time in months, she softened. "Then we can grow," she whispered.

Later, after the group dissolved and everyone left in twos or silence, Musa stayed behind. Tariq lingered.

"You okay?" he asked.

Musa nodded.

"No. But that's not the goal."

"What is?"

"Honesty. Even when it hurts. Especially then."

That night, Abe prayed maghrib. For the first time in weeks. He didn't say much after. Just held the sajdah long. As if apologizing with his forehead.

Hasan deleted his LinkedIn app. Took out his phone. Texted his little sister.

Hasan: "Can we FaceTime tomorrow? I miss you."

She replied in all caps: "WHO ARE YOU AND WHAT HAVE YOU DONE WITH MY BROTHER???"

He laughed. For real.

Tariq sat on his bed that night, staring at the ceiling. No music. No journal. No planning. Just breath. And the memory of Sonya's voice: *You don't need to be perfect. You just need to stay.*

The Name You Claim

They called it "The Circle 2.0." A half-joke, half-ritual born after their most honest gathering yet.

It was Abe's idea.

"Yo, if we're all dropping the fake stuff, let's rename ourselves."

"Rename?" Hasan asked. "Like legal?"

"Nah," Abe said, grinning. "Just a name you give yourself. One that tells the truth."

They gathered at the rooftop terrace of East Campus on a Sunday evening, the city humming below them like a living drum. Jackets pulled tight, steam rising from chipped coffee mugs, each of them holding a scrap of paper.

One by one, they spoke.

Michael went first. "My name is Baseem—the one who smiles. Because I finally let people see the parts of me I thought had to stay hidden."

He folded the paper and placed it in the bowl they'd brought.

Hasan followed. "My name is Najiy—the one who survives. Because I'm still here. Still breathing. Even when I forgot how to rest."

Abe stood next. "My name is Sadiq—truthful. Because I lied for so long just to be liked. And now... I just want to be real."

Rohan took a breath. "My name is Tameer—the one who builds. Even if I'm building from broken bricks."

Musa stood tall. "My name is Ghalib—the one who overcomes. Because I've been carrying legacy like a burden. And now, I carry it like a bridge."

They all looked at Tariq. He stood, hands in his pockets. "My name is

Nour—light. Not because I shine all the time. But because I finally stopped dimming for everyone else." He sat.

They turned to Sonya. She smiled. "I'll keep my name," she said. "But I'll add one." She pulled a folded paper from her sleeve. "Shajara. Tree. Because I've had to grow in too many storms. But I'm still rooted."

They all nodded. No applause. Just reverence.

Afterward, they returned to the dorm. No fireworks. No announcements. Just peace. Small, rare, hard-earned peace.

Tariq walked Sonya out. They stood near the dorm's side entrance, the wind tugging at the edges of their conversation.

"You surprised me," she said.

"How?"

"You listened. And you didn't try to fix it."

He smiled. "I'm learning silence might be its own kind of strength."

She looked down, then up. "You're becoming someone I might really trust."

He swallowed. "I want to be worthy of that."

They stood quietly.

Then she said, "You know this thing between us... it's complicated."

"I know."

"But it's real."

He nodded. "I won't chase you. But I'll never stop making space."

She blinked slowly. "Then maybe that's enough for now."

They didn't hug. Didn't kiss. But when she turned to go, he whispered: "Shajara."

She turned back, smiled, and whispered: "Nour."

And they walked in opposite directions—Not away. But forward.

Back upstairs, Musa wrote in his journal:

> *Today we named ourselves. Not because the world approved,*
> *but because the mirror demanded it. We will forget. We will*

falter. But now, we know where to return.

CHAPTER SEVEN

Smoke Without Fire

The Spark

It started with a flyer. One of those poorly designed, easily overlooked pieces of student activism that usually fade into the background of bulletin boards and Instagram stories. But this one hit different. Bold red letters. A black-and-white photo of a young hijabi woman, eyes covered by a censor bar. Below it: "Who's Protecting Muslim Women on This Campus?" A teach-in on patriarchy, piety politics, and the MSA's silence.

It was hosted by a new group—The Faith & Justice Collective, a mostly-female, multiracial crew of progressive students with ties to various activist circles. Some wore hijab. Some didn't. Some prayed. Some didn't. But they all had something to say. And Sonya? She was one of the speakers. Not the organizer. But not silent, either.

The flyer went viral in hours. Not just among Columbia students. It spread across intercollegiate Muslim group chats, reposted on TikTok and X (formerly Twitter) with captions like: "Finally calling out MSA hypocrisy," "Muslim women deserve safe space too," "Why is the MSA always led by brothers?" and "If you're uncomfortable, it's probably because it's true."

Some were supportive. Some were... not.

Tariq saw it mid-morning, between classes. He didn't even open the full post. The title alone was enough to punch the air out of his chest. He didn't text Sonya. Didn't know if he had the right anymore. But something inside him flared—not anger exactly. More like... betrayal's quieter cousin: disappointment. He thought they were building something. Something honest. Something whole. And now? Now her name was being mentioned in group chats with emojis he couldn't decipher.

Musa saw the flyer in the worst possible way: someone taped it to his dorm room door. He didn't touch it. Didn't even tear it down. Just stared at it for a full minute before folding it, quietly, and placing it inside his desk drawer. Then he sat. Hands folded. Back straight. And whispered a du'a he hadn't said since his first week on campus: "Ya Allah, make me invisible until I understand what to say."

The rest of the circle felt it immediately.

Abe messaged Tariq: "You seeing this flyer nonsense?"

Michael texted Rohan: "We're about to be collateral damage in someone else's revolution."

Hasan sent no messages. But his Google searches that night included: "How to issue a campus press statement," "What does defamation mean in New York State?" and "Can Muslims sue each other?"

The campus tension rose fast. People chose sides before conversations began. Some called it "necessary criticism." Others said it was "an internal matter turned into a performance." By Thursday, the MSA board released a carefully worded statement:

> *We hear the concerns being raised, and we are working internally to reflect and grow. Our spaces must center dignity, equity, and sincerity—especially for our sisters. We invite honest feedback but reject any framing that divides our ummah.*

It didn't help. Because people didn't want diplomacy. They wanted accountability. And more than a few wanted spectacle.

That night, the dorm was loud in all the wrong ways. Not with shouting. But with silence you could taste. Tariq paced the hallway. Musa sat in the lounge, Qur'an open but untouched. Rohan typed a paragraph. Deleted it. Typed again. Michael just kept saying: "We need a firewall. We need a plan."

Abe slammed a drawer. Hasan made a spreadsheet. No one slept.

Tariq finally broke the silence. He called Sonya. She answered.

"I didn't write the flyer," she said immediately. "I didn't even know they were using that title."

"But you're speaking," he replied. "I am."

"Why didn't you tell me?"

"I didn't think I needed permission."

Tariq's voice tightened. "It's not about permission. It's about trust. About knowing you're not throwing the rest of us under the bus for applause."

Sonya's tone stayed calm. "I'm not naming names. I'm naming patterns."

"And now everyone's watching us like we're suspects."

"They've been watching you," she said. "Now they're just saying it out loud."

That one hit too hard. He ended the call quietly. No yelling. Just... distance.

Later that night, he wrote in his journal:

> *Maybe this is what fire feels like when it's not trying to burn you—just trying to remind you there's smoke around the truths*

Divided at the Root

The group chat was on fire by 8 a.m.

Abe: "We need to issue a statement. Like, yesterday. This is getting out of hand. People think we're misogynists now. You see that meme of 'six haram bros and a microwave'? That's us."

Michael: "Tariq, check Twitter. ColumbiaConfessions is blowing up.

Someone posted screenshots of your old post about Black Muslim men needing their own spaces. They're twisting it."

Rohan: "If we say something now, it'll look defensive. Let it die out. Also... maybe parts of what they're saying aren't wrong."

Musa: (no response)

Hasan: "I have three drafts ready. One is soft. One is firm. One quotes Malcolm X and makes us look like a movement."

Tariq: "We're not a movement. We're a dorm of confused young Muslims who pray and eat chips and mess up."

Abe: "Exactly. Let's say that. Authentically. Before they define us for us."

Musa (finally): "I will not issue statements to please people who never prayed beside us."

And just like that, the split cracked wide.

Later that day, Musa skipped class. Instead, he walked across campus in silence, hands deep in his jacket pockets, earbuds in but no sound playing. He passed the main gates of Earl Hall, where the event would be held tomorrow night. The teach-in. The one Sonya was speaking at.

He stared at the flyers taped to the stone walls. A group of students stood nearby, laughing and snapping selfies in front of the event poster like it was a protest concert.

He turned around and left.

Not because he was angry. Because he was tired. Tired of being someone else's lesson. Tired of trying to prove that his dignity didn't come at the expense of anyone else's.

Back in the dorm, Abe was pacing the hallway. "Yo," he said to Michael. "I'm tweeting. Like, now. From my real account."

Michael didn't look up. "You sure?"

"I'm not about to be anyone's villain for existing. I've never disrespected a woman in my life."

"You sure about that?"

Abe froze.

Michael finally looked at him. "I'm saying... what we think is harmless often isn't."

Abe sighed. "I just... I feel judged. And I don't even know what I did."

Michael nodded. "Welcome to being seen through someone else's lens."

Rohan, meanwhile, had a plan. He wasn't interested in statements. He was interested in strategy. He opened his laptop, pulled up Canva, and began designing a new flyer:

> *"Faith, Brotherhood, and Accountability: A Town Hall with Columbia MSA." Hosted by the MSA Men's Council. Open to all. Listen first, speak after.*

He sent it directly to the MSA board. No approval needed. They posted it within the hour.

No one in the circle knew. Not yet.

Tariq spent the evening walking the perimeter of campus. From Amsterdam to Broadway. Up to 120th. Down to 110th. Every step felt like a delay.

Delay from having to choose. Because that's what it had come down to. Sonya. Musa. The Circle. The community. The truth.

He couldn't defend everyone. And he didn't know how to stand for one without feeling like he was betraying another.

He finally returned to the dorm, slipped past his brothers, and collapsed on his bed. His stayed closed.

At 11:57 p.m., Musa sent one final message to the group chat: "I'm not showing up to be cross-examined. If anyone wants to speak with me, do so directly. I won't perform my humanity in public."

No one responded. Not yet.

At 12:03 a.m., Michael texted Tariq separately: "You're gonna have to lead this one, bro. Not because you want to. But because you're the only one they'll still listen to."

Tariq stared at the message.

He didn't reply. He just sat with it. Like a name he didn't ask for. Like a weight he knew was already his.

The Fire Circle

The room was over capacity. Fold-out chairs lined the back wall. Students sat crisscrossed on the floor, backs against the cinderblock walls of Hamilton 602. Someone had brought samosas. Someone else had brought protest energy.

The air buzzed with heat—emotional, ideological, unspoken.

At the front stood a makeshift panel: five students, four of them women. A handwritten banner hung behind them, slightly crooked: "WHO'S PROTECTING MUSLIM WOMEN ON THIS CAMPUS?"

Musa didn't come. Neither did Hasan. But Tariq, Abe, Rohan, and Michael were there.

Not together. Scattered. Like witnesses too uncertain to sit side-by-side.

Sonya was the third speaker. She stepped up to the mic in a loose hoodie, jeans, and flats. No hijab tonight. Hair tied back. Earrings small. Energy... sharp, but not hostile.

She didn't read from notes. She just spoke.

"There's something about invisibility that teaches you to scan every room before you sit down."

Pause.

"I used to think modesty meant shrinking. That the less I took up space, the more sacred I became."

Another pause.

"I've unlearned that."

Nods from the crowd.

She continued. "I'm not here to cancel anyone. I'm here to ask why the places that claim to uplift us sometimes become the ones we fear the most."

She glanced at the crowd—not accusing, just... searching.

I've prayed beside brothers who won't look me in the eye but will still tell me how to live. I've been in MSA group chats where every flyer has brothers' names and every thank-you post forgets the women who ran the event."

Now some of the crowd clapped. Tariq's hands stayed folded.

"I'm not here because I hate Islam. I'm here because I love it too much to watch it become a mirror for patriarchy."

Silence. Respectful. She stepped back.

The moderator, a Somali sister in a maroon hijab, nodded. "Questions or reflections?"

A hand shot up. A white convert brother from Brooklyn. Junior. Political science major. Loud on Twitter. "I hear you. I agree with you. But where's the accountability? Where are the brothers from MSA? Don't they have anything to say?"

Tariq's chest tightened.

The crowd turned, slow as a tide. Eyes scanning the room. Searching for someone to stand.

Abe looked at Rohan.

Rohan looked at Michael.

Michael looked at Tariq.

Tariq closed his eyes for a second. And stood.

He walked to the front slowly. No fanfare. No pretense. Just presence.

He stepped to the mic. No notes. No script. Just breath.

"My name is Tariq Rahman," he began. "I'm a junior. Pre–social work."

He exhaled.

"I'm also one of the brothers who's been in every MSA meeting y'all are talking about."

The crowd tensed slightly.

He looked out—not at Sonya. At everyone.

"And I want to say two things. First, thank you. To every woman in this room who's been patient with our immaturity. Who's carried the weight of our silences. Who's served and cooked and planned and prayed while still being sidelined."

A few audible mm-hmms.

"Second... I'm sorry."

The room went still.

"I'm sorry for the ways we've centered ourselves. For the excuses we've made. For the times we let ego dress up like leadership." His voice cracked just slightly.

"I'm not the president of MSA. I'm not a scholar. I'm not a saint. I'm just... a guy who prays with his brothers and sometimes forgets that half the ummah is watching us forget them."

Sonya blinked once.

Tariq looked at her.

Then back at the crowd.

"And I'm not here to defend the MSA. Or explain away your pain. I'm here to ask: 'What do we build now?'"

The crowd was silent. But it was a full silence.

Not tension. Not fear. Listening.

Tariq nodded once. And stepped back.

Later, as the event ended, students milled around, buzzing. Some approached Sonya. Some approached Tariq. Few knew what to say.

Sonya walked up to him slowly.

"That was real," she said.

"I didn't come to be a hero."

"I know."

"But I couldn't stay quiet."

She nodded. "You weren't loud. You were honest. That's rarer."

He half-smiled. "You okay?" he asked.

She looked around the room. "Getting there."

"Need anything?"

"Just time."

"Take all of it."

That night, in his journal, Tariq wrote:

> *Today, we didn't win. We didn't fix. We didn't unify. But we showed up. And sometimes, presence is the first prayer.*

Embers

Musa waited until after Fajr to speak.

The dorm was still and half-lit, the city just starting to stretch its bones. Tariq sat alone in the lounge, eyes glazed from another sleepless night. A Qur'an lay open in front of him—but he hadn't turned a page in twenty minutes.

Musa entered silently, poured himself tea, and sat across from him.

For a while, he said nothing. Then: "She said a lot of truth."

Tariq looked up.

"But truth doesn't excuse framing," Musa added.

Tariq stayed still. "I know."

"She painted us as monoliths. As power-holders. As gatekeepers. I've spent my whole life trying not to be seen at all—and now I'm part of the problem?"

Tariq took a breath. "I don't think she was talking about you, Musa. I think she was talking about what we allow."

Musa's jaw clenched. "But when has anyone ever allowed me?"

He leaned forward. "I am not the enemy. I am the quiet son. The refugee's descendant. The prayer leader with imposter syndrome. I memorized the Qur'an not for status—but so I could feed my village with my degree one day. And now I'm the oppressor?"

Tariq didn't interrupt.

Musa's voice cracked. "She stood in a room of strangers and made us the backdrop for her liberation arc. And yes, maybe some of it was needed. But it made me feel... used."

That word hung heavy. Then: "I'm tired of being the misunderstood savior. I want to just... be."

Tariq nodded. "Then let's figure out what that looks like. Together."

By noon, the rest of the group had gathered in the dorm lounge.

Abe was pacing.

Michael was quiet but present.

Rohan had a new folder labeled "Post-Controversy Recovery Doc."

Hasan walked in last, holding printouts.

"I've been thinking," he said. "We need to build something new. Something not tied to MSA, or to this dorm, or to what people think we are."

Michael raised an eyebrow. "Like... a new org?"

"No. A new circle. A new name. Something decentralized. Built on mutual growth. Events. Conversations. Real space for faith and failure."

Abe nodded. "I'm down."

Rohan tilted his head. "Who leads it?"

"That's the point," Hasan replied. "No one. Or... everyone."

Musa looked up. "That only works if ego dies first."

Rohan shot back, "And silence doesn't equal submission."

The tension crackled.

Then Abe stood. "Nah. If we're doing this, we gotta do it clean. Real rules. Real trust."

He looked at Rohan. "I love you, bro. But you're still out here trying to be right more than you're trying to heal."

Rohan folded his arms. "And you're still trying to fix everything with jokes and passion."

Michael held up a hand. "Or maybe we're all trying to protect something we haven't even named yet."

Hasan said, "We're not here to save Columbia."

Tariq, finally speaking, added: "We're here to save each other."

Later that evening, after the meeting dissolved into long silences and nods of agreement, Tariq walked Sonya home.

They didn't talk much. Just moved side by side beneath the cold canopy of campus trees, the wind tugging at their sleeves.

At her building, she stopped. "You handled that event like a grown man."

Tariq smirked. "I cried in the bathroom after."

"Still counts."

They stood in the threshold of goodbye.

She looked up. "I'm proud of you."

"I'm proud of you too."

Then she hesitated. "There's a world where we're... more."

Tariq didn't look away. "And this isn't that world?"

She smiled, gently. "It might be. But I'm not ready to walk into it yet."

He nodded. "Then I'll be wherever you are. As a friend. As your witness."

That word made her blink. *Witness.*

She kissed his cheek.

"Goodnight, Nour."

"Goodnight, Shajara."

And she was gone.

Back in the dorm, Tariq opened his journal.

> *The fire didn't burn us down. It revealed where the cracks were. And now? Now we rebuild. Not with ego. Not with image. But with intention.*

After the Smoke

They met in the dorm lounge again, just after Isha.

No MSA name tags. No chairs in neat rows. No flyer. No hashtags. No snacks. Just bodies on the floor. Shoes off. Backs straight. Souls sore, but present.

It was Abe who spoke first. "So... what now?"

Michael answered. "We build. One moment at a time."

They nodded.

Tariq pulled out a notebook and flipped to a blank page. Not to take minutes. Just to mark the moment.

"Alright," he said. "Let's start small. What do we want this to feel like?"

Hasan: "Safe."

Rohan: "Unpolished."

Abe: "Honest, even when it's ugly."

Michael: "Non-digital. No recording. Just presence."

Musa: "Prayerful. But not performative."

Tariq: "Ours."

They sat with that. Then they listed:

- No hierarchy.
- No speeches.
- No saving face.
- No shaming.
- Everyone listens.
- Everyone confesses.
- Everyone shows up.

Musa added, "We don't just vent. We act. If someone's slipping, we reach."

Rohan asked, "But who holds us accountable?"

Tariq responded: "The circle."

Abe grinned. "That sounds kinda culty."

They all laughed. Musa smiled.

Then Abe added, "But like... the good kind of cult."

Hasan pulled out a folded sticky note. "I wrote this a while ago. Didn't know what it was for."

He placed it in the center of the circle.

Written in bold black ink: "We rise when no one is watching."

Michael nodded. "That's it."

They sat in silence for a few minutes. No one rushed to close. No one wrapped it up with a prayer. They just breathed.

As they prepared to leave, Tariq stayed behind.

Musa lingered.

"I almost left," he said quietly. "All of it. The MSA. Columbia. Even the city."

Tariq didn't respond. He just waited.

"But I didn't," Musa continued. "Because something told me... this was still holy. Even in its brokenness."

Tariq looked him in the eyes. "It still is."

They bumped fists. No hugs. Just pressure and permission in one gesture.

That night, as each of them returned to their rooms, something soft settled into their bones.

Not pride. Not closure. But a sense that something had finally begun.

Tariq opened his journal and wrote the first line of a new entry:

We are not what they said. We are not what we feared. We are what remains when the fire clears—and the floor still holds.

He stared at the page. Then wrote:

The Circle We Made, October 27, 2001, Columbia University

And under that:

Let this be our beginning.

CHAPTER EIGHT

Proof of Life

Where the Breath Settles

It had been two weeks since the Circle was reborn. Not announced. Not declared. Just lived into.

The brothers had stopped calling it meetings.

There were no RSVPs. No carpeted schedules. No formal plans.

But every Wednesday after Isha, they gathered. Quietly. Sometimes to talk. Sometimes just to sit.

There was a new rhythm now. Not loud. But present.

Tariq noticed it first in his own body. His shoulders had dropped. His gait was slower. His eyes didn't scan rooms for tension like they used to.

He had switched majors officially. Social work. With a concentration in community organizing.

It felt right. But with that peace came questions.

Would his parents understand? Would his father—who still introduced him as "my son, the future attorney"—see him now as anything but a deviation?

He hadn't told them yet. Not fully. The tuition check had cleared, so he knew the truth hadn't reached home. But it would. And when it did... He didn't know what would survive the collision.

Michael was the second to change. Subtly.

He began building something. Not a website. Not an app.

A curriculum. With Hasan.

They met in the Butler Library basement twice a week, surrounded by reference books and untouched whiteboards.

They drafted modules:

- One on emotional intelligence and Muslim masculinity
- One on healthy disagreement in Islamic tradition
- One on unlearning shame through faith

They didn't say it out loud, but both knew: this was the Circle's first offering.

Not just gatherings. Not just venting. But tools.

Michael coded in silence.

Hasan took notes like he was preparing to speak at the United Nations.

Neither said it, but both believed: this wasn't for Columbia alone.

This could go further.

Someday.

Meanwhile, Rohan had started walking past the pharmacy building more than usual. He never admitted it, even to himself. But once or twice a week, his route to class just... shifted.

Aisha didn't reach out. And he didn't know if he could.

But that didn't stop the remembering.

How she challenged his business metaphors. How she always left space for silence. How she told him once: "I'd rather be alone with truth than partnered with performance."

He wasn't sure he was ready to live that yet. But the thought stayed with him. Like a bookmark on a page, he wasn't done reading.

Abe? He was everywhere.

Dorm lounges. Events. Halal food trucks.

He became the unofficial ambassador of the Circle—telling people without telling them.

Not to recruit. Just to signal. To say, "There's a space where we're not pretending."

But that energy? It rubbed Musa the wrong way.

One night, after a long post-Jumu'ah dinner, Musa pulled him aside.

"You're turning this into a stage," he said.

Abe blinked. "Nah, bro. I'm just repping. Letting people know it's safe."

"There's a difference between invitation and advertisement."

Abe crossed his arms. "Why are you mad that people are excited?"

Musa didn't raise his voice. "I'm not mad. I'm protective. Some things aren't built for the spotlight."

Abe leaned forward. "And some things die in the dark."

They stood there, the tension thick.

Finally, Abe said, "Maybe we just have different ideas of what sincerity looks like."

Musa replied, "Maybe."

But his eyes said: *You're not wrong. But neither am I.*

Back in the dorm that night, Tariq sat in the hallway between both their rooms. Neither came out.

He didn't force it. He just sat there, legs out, head back, listening to the hum of the vending machine and the low echo of someone laughing two floors down.

Then he pulled out his journal.

> *A circle only holds when each corner learns it was never the center.*

He closed it. Breathed deep. Waited.

Just in case one of them opened the door.

Fractures of Faith

Musa hadn't spoken Wolof in weeks. Not in full sentences. Not in feeling.

Most of the time, he whispered it in du'a. Or thought it silently when he missed home. Or read it in the letter his mother wrote last Eid, folded into the crease of his Qur'an.

But when he opened the door and saw Bakary—his childhood friend from Gambia—standing in the hallway of Columbia's dorms, smiling wide and already pulling him into a hug, the language poured out.

"Waw, Musa, look at you! Beard shining like a scholar. You look fat with American comfort!"

Musa laughed, genuinely for the first time in days. "Wallahi, you haven't changed."

"And you? You've become one of them," Bakary teased. "Tight jeans, earbuds, phone always buzzing. I almost didn't recognize you."

They sat in the lounge. No one else around.

Bakary was in town for a cultural exchange fellowship—a one-week series of student panels between Senegalese, Gambian, and American undergrads. He'd been selected because of his leadership in a youth development program back home.

"I tell the kids all the time," Bakary said proudly, "that you are our North Star. I say, 'Musa went to America and still remembers who he is.'"

Musa smiled, but it didn't reach his eyes. Because he didn't know if that was true anymore.

They talked for hours. About their village. Their old imam. The soccer field with one good net. The mango tree where they used to skip Qur'an class to eat stolen fruit.

But then the questions came. "When will you return to teach?" "When will you send a proper donation? Not just one-time sadaqah but real help?" "Are you still praying five times a day?" "Are you still reciting like we used to? Or has the city softened your voice?"

Musa answered politely. Then firmly. Then... quietly.

Later, when Bakary left for the campus hotel, Musa didn't go back to his room. He went to the masjid. Sat on the carpet alone. Stared at the empty rows. Then whispered: "Ya Allah... How do I serve the people who raised me without erasing the person I'm still becoming?"

The answer didn't come. But neither did judgment. Just the sound of the heater rumbling. The building breathing.

Musa placed his forehead to the carpet. And stayed there. Not praying. Just being.

Meanwhile, across campus, Tariq was standing outside Dodge Hall when his phone rang. The number was local but unknown. He hesitated. Then answered.

"Is this Brother Tariq Rahman?"

The voice was deep. Polite. Older.

"Yes, this is him."

"This is Imam Siraj Uddin from the Masjid Muhammad Initiative. We've heard about your recent speak-out on campus. About the Circle."

Tariq blinked. "From who?"

"People are paying attention. Your name's being mentioned. Some of us... are listening."

He didn't know what to say.

The imam continued.

"We'd like to invite you to join our new mentorship council. Help us build a citywide Muslim youth program."

"I'm still a student."

"Exactly. We need people who know what it feels like to struggle in the now. Not just scholars who speak from ten years removed."

Tariq ran a hand over his face.

"What's the commitment?"

"Monthly. Hybrid. We meet in Harlem. We need visionaries. Not saviors."

That line hit hard.

He told the imam he'd think about it.

Hung up.

Stared at the skyline.

And whispered, "Why now?"

Not because he was afraid. But because he wanted it. And that scared him.

Back in the dorm that night, Musa finally returned. Tariq was in the hallway, reading. They nodded to each other. But didn't speak. Not yet.

They didn't need to. Because faith is not just prayer and recitation. Sometimes faith is walking past the memory of who you were—

and still choosing to stay where you are.

Tariq later wrote:

> *Faith is not certainty. It's the breath between questions. The silence between answers. The pause before "Ameen."*

Gentle Collisions

Rohan hadn't planned to see her.

He told himself he was just going to pick up some notes from the health sciences library. A quick visit. No detours.

But as he turned the corner near the anatomy labs, he saw her.

Aisha.

Hair wrapped in a soft gold scarf. Lab coat folded neatly over her arm. Eyes slightly tired, but still sharp enough to see him from across the hallway.

She didn't stop walking.

She just smiled. "Hi, Rohan."

It hit like a whisper that still echoed.

"Hey," he said.

They stood in the hallway like actors who'd forgotten their lines.

Then she broke the silence.

"You surviving?"

"Barely," he joked. "You?"

"Still breathing. Med school doesn't kill you—it just slowly steals your joy in manageable units."

He laughed. A real one. The wall between them softened by a few bricks.

"Can I walk you out?" he asked.

She nodded.

They didn't talk about the past. Not directly. They talked about exams. Cafeteria food. How Columbia smelled worse after rain than any other Ivy League campus.

Then she stopped walking and turned to face him.

"I read the flyer," she said.

He blinked. "The Circle event?"

She nodded. "The one with your name listed as co-organizer."

"I didn't even plan to be public with it."

"But you are."

He swallowed. "Do you think it's performative?"

"I think it's necessary."

Pause.

"But it's only real if you're still that person when the room empties."

He nodded. "I'm trying."

Aisha looked at him. Long. Quiet.

"I believe that."

She turned to go. He didn't stop her.

But before she disappeared into the crowd, she turned back.

"If you ever want to talk... with no expectations, no pressure—just presence—I'm around."

He exhaled.

"I might take you up on that."

She smiled once. Then walked away.

Back in the dorm lounge that evening, Abe burst into the room like a storm with a purpose.

"Alright, y'all—don't kill me, but hear this out."

Tariq looked up.

Michael lowered his laptop lid.

Musa raised an eyebrow.

Hasan paused his tea steep.

"I think we should host an open mic night."

Silence.

"With poetry, spoken word, comedy, testimony. No filters. No vibe policing. Just... voices."

More silence.

Then: "Why?"

"Because the world thinks Muslims are either angry or perfect," Abe said. "Let's show them we're complicated. Let's show them we're real."

Musa rubbed his temples. "Or we could just pray quietly and not open the door to *fitnah*."

Hasan added, "You do realize this will attract every critic, troll, and youth group watchdog within a ten-mile radius?"

Michael said, "We'll need guidelines."

Rohan, quietly entering the room, said: "We'll need boundaries too. Not just rules."

Tariq didn't speak. Not yet. He just watched them argue. Not with venom. But with fire.

The kind of fire that meant they cared. He finally stood.

"If we do this," he said, "we're not doing it to impress. Or defend. Or perform."

He looked around.

"We do it because the Circle isn't a brand. It's a bridge."

Musa met his eyes. "And a bridge is only holy if it holds."

Abe smirked. "So... we're doing it?"

Michael nodded. "If we curate it right."

Hasan said, "If we prepare spiritually. Not just logistically."

Tariq closed his notebook.

"Then let's make space for truth—without selling our souls for applause."

Later that night, Tariq walked alone near the edge of campus, scrolling through emails.

The subject line on one caught his eye: "Community Leadership Summit – Panel Invitation: Youth and Faith"

Another spotlight. Another room he didn't ask to stand in. He closed the email.

Not because he didn't want it. But because he wanted to stay centered before saying yes to the world again.

In his journal that night, he wrote:

> *The danger isn't in being seen. The danger is forgetting who you are when the light hits your face.*

The Weight of Witness

Michael hadn't planned to speak.

He came to the Wednesday Circle the same way he always did—quiet, hoodie on, legs crossed, notebook open but rarely touched. He liked it that way. Believed his presence was contribution enough.

But when Abe commented—half-joke, half-confession—about "never being able to open up to your family without it turning into a lecture or a guilt trip," Michael exhaled harder than he meant to.

And they noticed.

Tariq looked over. "You feel that?"

Michael shrugged

Then said, quietly, "My parents still think I'm majoring in engineering."

The room stilled.

"I switched last semester. Computer science with a psych minor. Didn't tell them."

Musa blinked. "Why not?"

"Because my father spent twelve years telling me tech was just a stepping stone to real success. And my mom... she just wants peace. Not waves."

Rohan asked, gently, "So you're lying to them?"

Michael nodded. "By omission. By performance. By silence."

Abe said, "Yo, that's wild. You show up for everyone here."

Michael looked down.

"That's the problem. I built myself around being useful. Predictable. Silent. And now... I don't know how to be loved without proving something first."

No one spoke. Not because they didn't know what to say. But because they knew exactly what he meant.

Musa reached across the circle. Not with words. Just with his hand. Palm up.

Michael hesitated.

Then placed his own in his. No grip. No squeeze. Just presence.

That night, Musa dreamed in color. It was home. The well he used to draw water from. The field where he learned to ride a donkey. His grandfather's voice reciting Qur'an at dawn. His mother frying fish over an open flame.

But in the dream, the well was dry. He climbed down, searching. And at the bottom, he found a mirror—cracked down the middle.

He lifted it and saw his own face split between two versions: On the left, the man with tired eyes and city weight. On the right, a boy in a white thawb, wide-eyed, soft-handed.

He woke up sweating. And whispered, "Ya Allah... help me be both."

That Friday, the brothers sat around a chalkboard in the campus ministry center. Planning the open mic. Not the aesthetics. The intention.

"What do we want people to leave with?" Hasan asked.

Rohan: "Permission to be real."

Abe: "And a sense that they're not alone in their contradictions."

Musa scribbled one line at the top of the board: Not perfect. Just honest.

Michael looked at it and said, "We're not planning an event."

Tariq nodded. "We're planning a witness."

Hasan looked up. "A what?"

Tariq folded his arms. "Every prophet was a witness before he was a preacher. He showed up. He named the truth. He held space for what people didn't want to say."

Abe grinned. "You're really leaning into this whole leadership thing, huh?"

Tariq laughed. "I'm not leading. I'm just... trying not to disappear."

That night, after everyone left, Musa stayed behind. Erased the chalkboard slowly. Then added one last line at the bottom: We rise not to be seen. We rise to see each other.

He stepped back. Exhaled. And whispered, "Bismillah."

The Night Before the Mic

The chalkboard was full. Not with to-do lists. With names. Each brother had written the name of a person they wished could hear tomorrow's open mic. Not attend. Just hear. Musa wrote his mother. Michael wrote his younger self. Hasan wrote, "any kid in a masjid corner scared to cry." Abe wrote a name, then quickly erased it. Rohan wrote no one—but his hand lingered on the chalk longer than the others. And Tariq wrote "Baba." Not Dad. Not Father. Baba. And then he sat back like he wasn't sure why.

The nerves didn't show until 11 p.m. That's when Abe started pacing.

That's when Hasan asked if they needed liability waivers. That's when Rohan checked the sign-up sheet four times in a row. That's when Michael said, "What if this is a mistake?"

And that's when Tariq's phone buzzed. Unknown number. But he recognized it instantly.

Baba: Heard you're organizing something. Saw it on a WhatsApp group. People are talking. Good luck.

No "I'm proud of you." No "We'll be watching." Just: People are talking. Tariq stared at the screen. Then placed it face down.

An hour later, while scrolling through anonymous submissions on their open mic RSVP form, he received a voice note. From Sonya. He hesitated. Then pressed play. Her voice was calm. Quiet. Recorded outside—he could hear wind and maybe traffic in the background.

"I'm not coming tomorrow. Not because I don't support it. But because I think this space is for something I no longer need to prove I belong to. That said..."

A pause.

"...I'm proud of you. For building what didn't exist. For not giving in to performance. And for showing up anyway—even when you weren't sure it would hold."

Another pause.

"Just promise me this: no matter how many people clap—remember why you started. And who you're still becoming."

The message ended. Tariq didn't replay it. He didn't need to.

Back in the dorm, the brothers gathered one final time before the mic. No prep talk. No speeches. Just prayer. One rak'ah. Then a circle.

Musa sat up straight.

"We say bismillah not because we're ready. But because we know we need Allah."

Michael added, "And each other."

Abe passed around sticky notes. "For pockets. Write your intention. Keep it close."

They scribbled in silence. Then Tariq stood. Not to lead. Just to offer the only sentence that felt honest: "We're not about to perform. We're about to witness. And witnessing isn't loud. It's sacred."

They nodded. Then they folded their notes. Pressed them into their chests. And said "Ameen."

Back in his room, Tariq opened his journal. He didn't write a poem. He didn't write a prayer. He just wrote the title of tomorrow's event. Not Perfect. Just Honest. Under it:

We are not poets. We are not prophets. We are young men with burning lungs, trying to breathe honesty into a world that holds its breath when we speak.

CHAPTER NINE

Not Perfect, Just Honest

The Room Fills Slowly

The chairs were mismatched. Some metal. Some wood. Some borrowed from other student org lounges. One was a desk chair someone had wheeled in from a nearby hallway.

There were no stage lights. No DJ booth. Just two standing lamps from a resale app, pointed at a handmade wooden stool and a single mic stand.

But the space—room 501, Hamilton Hall—felt alive. Because it wasn't built to impress. It was built to hold truth.

Tariq arrived an hour early, hoodie up, clipboard in hand—not because he needed to organize, but because he needed something to hold.

Michael checked the sound system.

Abe triple-checked the snacks.

Rohan lit a cheap candle and placed it under the stool, jokingly calling it their "intention flame."

Hasan, normally composed, was silent. He kept pulling out his phone, checking his GPA tracker app, and slipping it away again like an unholy ritual.

Musa sat cross-legged by the far wall, eyes closed, whispering quiet dhikr.

No one said it out loud, but the room was heavy with breath.

Like it knew this was no regular night.

By 6:32 p.m., students began trickling in.

Some came for the poetry. Some came for the controversy. Some just needed a place to feel something they hadn't been able to name yet.

The Circle had set clear guidelines:

- No recording
- No judgment
- No heckling
- Snap or tap if you feel it
- Leave if you must, but don't pretend you didn't hear what was said

At 6:45, the first surprise arrived: Professor Akhtar. Tariq saw him from across the room, wearing his usual navy sweater and carrying a folded newspaper under one arm.

He nodded at Tariq like this was office hours and the world wasn't about to watch him unspool. Tariq's chest tightened. He hadn't invited him. But of course, he came. That's what witnesses do.

Then came a second surprise. Aisha. She entered quietly, no fanfare. Sat near the back. Rohan noticed. He didn't speak. Just straightened in his seat like his posture was an apology.

And then a third surprise. Not a person. A message. Hasan's phone buzzed. He checked it. Froze.

Tariq, catching the shift, walked over.

"You good?"

Hasan nodded too fast.

Then said, quietly: "My academic advisor just sent me a warning flag."

Tariq blinked. "What kind of warning?"

"I'm two points from probation. Midterm grades dropped. He wants to 'discuss my capacity to maintain full enrollment.'"

Tariq's stomach sank. "You didn't say anything."

"Didn't want to be the weak link," Hasan said.

Tariq placed a hand on his shoulder. "You're the one who holds half this circle together."

Hasan looked down. "Then pray I don't fall apart mid-semester."

At 6:58 p.m., the lights dimmed. Abe stepped forward—not loud, just present. He didn't announce. He didn't welcome.

He said: "Tonight's mic is open. But this space isn't empty. It's full of stories you haven't heard yet. Some of them are yours. Some of them might scare you. All of them deserve breath."

Pause.

"Not perfect. Just honest."

And with that, he stepped aside. And the first poet walked to the mic.

Tariq sat at the side of the room, notebook closed. No stage. No barrier. Just a room full of people watching a stool like it might levitate.

And in that moment, he thought: We built this. But we didn't build it for applause. We built it because truth has been silent too long.

Voices in the Flame

The first performer was a soft-spoken hijabi freshman named Layla.

She walked to the mic like she was delivering a tray of tea—steady, quiet, intentional.

She wore jeans under her abaya and clutched a paper so wrinkled it looked like it had been folded and unfolded a hundred times.

She didn't look up when she began. Just read.

> *"When I said I wanted to be seen,*
> *I didn't mean stared at.*
> *I meant held—*
> *like the moment after sujood,*
> *when breath hasn't come back yet*

but peace already has."

The room froze. She continued.

"When I told my mother I was tired,
she told me to pray.
When I told my advisor I was tired,
she told me to sleep.
When I told myself I was tired,
I just kept going."

She looked up. Eyes scanning the crowd, but not begging for response.

"I don't want to be strong anymore.
I want to be carried
by something holy,
and still call it mine."

She stepped back. Didn't wait for applause. Didn't nod. Just returned to her seat and cried quietly into her sleeves.

No one clapped. They just snapped. One by one. As if afraid to break the spell.

Musa wiped his eyes without letting anyone see.

Michael just nodded into his chest like he had been seen by something without form.

Hasan scribbled the word carried in his notebook and circled it three times.

Abe stood.

Tariq blinked. He hadn't signed up.

But now he was walking toward the mic like he didn't know he was doing it until he stood behind it.

Abe took the mic out of the stand.

Held it like a secret.

"Yo," he said.

No jokes. No jokes.

"Most people know me as the clown. The connector. The hype man."

Pause.

"But I'm also the brother who hasn't prayed Fajr on time in a month."

Silence.

"I'm the guy who says 'alhamdulillah' in the group chat and then texts a girl 'wyd' ten minutes later."

Murmurs. He laughed. One time. But it wasn't funny.

"I talk a lot because silence reminds me how alone I used to feel. Back when I didn't know if I was lovable without a punchline."

He looked at Musa. "Some of y'all think I'm playing games. But the truth is—this smile was built on survival."

He looked down. Back up.

"And I'm done surviving. I want to live. With God. With y'all. With myself."

He nodded. One time.

"Not perfect. Just honest."

He stepped back. And the room... didn't breathe for three seconds. Then erupted in the softest thunder imaginable.

Snaps. Taps. Two hands over hearts. One quiet "Ameen."

Back in their section, Musa leaned toward Tariq.

"He meant every word."

Tariq nodded. "But he's bleeding in front of strangers."

"That's what the prophets did," Musa replied.

"And look what it cost them."

In the back row, Rohan stared at his phone. Aisha had texted.

"I'm proud of your friend. That took real courage."

He typed back: "He's not the only one learning how to be honest."

He didn't hit send. Not yet.

Michael whispered to Hasan. "You okay?"

Hasan nodded too fast.

Michael narrowed his eyes. "You're not."

Hasan closed his notebook.

"I'm just calculating how much honesty I can afford without losing what I'm barely holding."

Michael didn't push.

Just said: "You don't owe the room everything. But you owe yourself something."

Back at the mic, a young man from NYU was reading about his uncle's deportation.

A girl from Queens rapped a piece about being Black, Muslim, and always mistaken for the help.

Someone read a love letter to the masjid they no longer felt safe in.

The stories kept coming.

Soft. Fierce. Holy.

Tariq didn't speak. Not yet. But the words were building behind his ribs like water behind a dam.

Something wanted to break. But he didn't know what.

In his notebook, he wrote:

> *I think God is in this room. Not because of the prayers, but because of the trembling before and after them.*

The Breaking Point

The boy was shaking before he reached the mic.

Tariq noticed it first.

He was a sophomore, maybe. Thin. Afghan-American. Big hoodie, nervous hands. His name tag said Haris.

He unfolded his paper with trembling fingers. Didn't look up.

He began.

"When my father found my journal, he didn't yell. He cried."

His voice cracked.

"When I told him I was scared of who I was becoming, he said: 'Then stop becoming it.'"

He paused. His breathing got louder. Faster.

"When I tried to pray, my hands shook too much to hold the tasbih. When I tried to fast, my hunger turned into hate. When I tried to speak, I lied."

He stopped. Froze. Then dropped the paper. And whispered into the mic: "I don't know if God still wants me."

Silence. Complete. Not a gasp. Not a rustle. Just stillness.

His voice broke again. "And I'm so tired of pretending that He does."

Then he stepped back. Tears streaming.

Someone moved to help him. But he raised one hand as if to say: Let me leave with dignity.

And he walked off. No claps. No snaps. Just presence. In the stunned quiet, the mic stood alone. Until Tariq stood.

No hesitation. No paper. No performance. Just... movement.

He walked up slowly. The room turned. He didn't touch the mic. He just looked at it. Then looked at them.

Then said: "There are some rooms where truth can't be clapped for. Where the silence after the sentence is the healing."

He let that breathe.

"Tonight isn't about perfection. And it's not about performance. It's about permission. To be whole. To be messy. To be halfway faithful and still belong."

He took a step closer.

"I don't know Haris. But I saw God in his honesty. And if we can't hold each other in that... then the circle we made means nothing."

Someone whispered Ameen.

Tariq turned to the mic. Spoke a final line: "You're still wanted. Even when you don't feel wanted."

He stepped back. And sat down.

Not to applause. But to breath returning to the room.

In the back, Haris sat with his head down.

Sonya had found him. She hadn't planned to come. But something told her the room needed witnesses.

She placed a hand on his shoulder. Said nothing. And stayed.

Michael scribbled in his notebook:

> *We don't save each other by speaking. We save each other by not running when the pain comes out loud.*

Musa bowed his head. Whispered a du'a so quietly only Allah could translate it.

And Tariq sat, shaking now, too. Not from fear. But from knowing—They would never be the same after this.

The Glow After

They didn't leave right away. No one did.

After the final piece, there was no emcee wrap-up. No obligatory thank-you speech. No group photo.

Just... stillness.

People sat in their chairs like they weren't sure if their legs could carry what their hearts were holding. Some hugged without asking. Others cried quietly into sleeves or notebook margins. A few strangers exchanged numbers—not for networking, but for healing check-ins.

The mic remained unplugged. The stool untouched. The candle under the stool still flickering, like it knew what it had just witnessed.

Musa found Haris before he left.

Didn't say much. Just pressed a slip of paper into his hand. On it: a single Qur'an verse and a time for Fajr the next morning.

Haris looked at it like a rope thrown into deep water. He nodded. Didn't smile. Just... nodded.

Michael and Rohan started gathering the chairs without being asked.

Abe was quiet, unusually so.

He wasn't drained. He was centered—like something he didn't even know he was praying for had just been answered.

Hasan sat with his back against the wall, eyes closed. Whispering dhikr under his breath like it was the only thing holding him together.

Maybe it was.

Tariq helped blow out the candle. He stood in the middle of the room, watching the slow tide of students exit.

Then he saw Sonya. She wasn't speaking. Just observing. Half-smiling.

He walked to her slowly.

She said, "That boy broke my heart."

Tariq replied, "He baptized the room in truth."

They stood quietly.

Sonya added, "You didn't perform tonight. You witnessed."

Tariq looked down. "I didn't know what to say."

"That's why it worked."

She stepped closer.

"You held the space. Even when it shook."

Tariq looked her in the eyes. "Thanks for coming."

"I wasn't going to. But then I realized—if this is what y'all are building, I want to know how to hold it too."

He nodded. "It's fragile."

She smiled. "So are most holy things."

And then she left. No hug. No promise. Just presence.

Back in the dorm, the brothers didn't say much. They sat in a loose circle on the floor. Musa made tea without asking. Michael passed around dates. Rohan laid flat on the carpet like he'd just finished a marathon.

Tariq finally said: "We didn't just host an event tonight. We made room."

Hasan whispered, "And we filled it."

They closed the night with one *rak'ah*.

No imam. Just breath syncing in surrender. And when they said *Ameen*, it wasn't just a prayer. It was a promise.

Tariq's journal that night:

> *The mic is silent now. But I still hear them—the voices that refused to stay hidden, the hearts that unraveled and rethreaded themselves in public. We are not a movement. We are not a miracle. We are a room that stayed even after the lights went off.*

CHAPTER TEN

What Follows the Fire

The Morning After Being Seen

The first message hit Tariq's inbox at 7:02 a.m. Subject line: "Last night was powerful. Thank you."

Then came another. "I've never felt so seen in a room of Muslims before."

Then another. "Y'all didn't just start a movement—you started a mirror."

By 7:30, he had 16 emails.

By 8:00, 42. By 9:00, a text from his advisor: "Impressive showing last night. Care to meet for coffee and discuss leadership potential?"

By 9:15, he had his head in his hands.

Across campus, the impact had already begun to ripple.

Hasan woke up to an email from the Office of Student Development: "Would you be open to consulting on a new interfaith initiative? We're hoping to center more Muslim voices."

He closed the email. Then opened his midterm grades again. And felt the crack grow.

Musa skipped breakfast. Not out of guilt. Out of preservation. He didn't want to hear what people "loved" about last night. Didn't want to be complimented for what should've been a given.

He opened his Qur'an instead. Found the verse about Allah knowing what's hidden in the breasts. Closed the book.

Then whispered, "Protect me from the applause I haven't earned."

Abe was glowing.

He walked through campus like his name had just been cleared on a billboard.

People stopped him. Snapbacks nodded. Sisters smiled.

Someone called out, "Spoken word legend!"

He grinned, of course. But later, in the library bathroom, he stared at his own reflection and asked, "Was I honest... or just loud?"

Michael received a DM from a former high school classmate: "Yo. Saw the video. You snapped. Didn't know you had it in you."

He stared at the message. They'd posted a clip. Someone had recorded Abe's set—despite the rules.

He checked the hashtag: #NotPerfectJustHonest It was already trending locally. His stomach turned.

Rohan got a message from Aisha. "Still sitting with last night. Something shifted."

He replied. "Same. Still not sure how to name it."

She sent back one line: "Sometimes names aren't the point. Presence is."

He didn't reply.

He just reread it five times.

Back in the dorm lounge, they began to gather again. Not planned. Just drawn together. Michael sat cross-legged, eyes on his phone.

Hasan entered, clearly exhausted.

Musa had prayer beads in one hand, coffee in the other.

Abe came in like he'd been waiting for this all day.

Tariq entered last.

Everyone looked at him.

He sat on the armrest of the couch.

Let the silence breathe.

Then said: "Y'all feel that?"

Michael nodded. "Too much."

Abe said, "We're legends now."

Musa murmured, "May Allah forgive us."

Hasan: "I'm getting praise from the same people who wouldn't share our last event flyer."

Tariq leaned forward.

"We told people not to record. Someone did anyway. The internet has it now."

Abe winced.

Musa looked down.

Michael whispered, "This is what happens when fire catches wind."

Rohan finally entered, laptop in hand.

Sat without a word.

Tariq looked at all of them.

"I think we need to decide—are we still a circle... or are we becoming something else?"

No one answered right away. But the question stayed in the room like incense smoke—light, fragrant, and unignorable.

Tariq's journal that night:

> *The mic is off. But the volume hasn't lowered. People are watching. Waiting to see if we were real or just dramatic. I didn't do this for followers. But now I feel followed. Ya Allah... protect our sincerity from our spotlight.*

With Praise Comes Pressure

It started with an email from Columbia's Office of Spiritual Life. "We'd love to feature you as the student voice of our new interfaith campaign. A video series. Maybe a TEDx-style talk. You'd be perfect."

Tariq didn't open it right away. He just stared at the subject line for two full minutes, thumb hovering, throat tight. It felt less like an invitation. More like an expectation.

Later that day, he bumped into Professor Akhtar outside of Butler Library.

"Rahman," the professor said, eyes warm behind thick glasses. "You realize you shook something loose the other night, yes?"

Tariq smiled nervously. "Wasn't trying to shake. Just speak."

"That's the same thing," Akhtar replied. "Come by my office. I have someone I'd like you to meet. An alum. Foundation donor. Big on 'narrative equity.' I think they'd see themselves in you."

Tariq nodded. Then walked away with lead in his stomach.

At the same time, Musa was back in the masjid library. Alone. Scrolling through stories and videos under the hashtag #NotPerfectJustHonest.

The comments poured in.

"This is the new generation of Muslims."

"Finally, brothers who cry."

"My masjid needs this energy."

He read them all. Then closed the browser. Then opened his Qur'an. Then closed that too. And whispered: "Ya Allah, am I part of something beautiful? Or just something popular?"

He didn't get an answer. But he didn't expect one.

Abe had been invited to a spoken word night hosted by a local activist collective. He said yes immediately. Walked in like he was a guest of honor. He wore a kufi tilted slightly to the side. Hoodie crisp. Chain tucked halfway in.

The piece he performed was... powerful. But loud. Less prayer, more performance. More bars than breath.

The crowd clapped hard. But Musa, who had quietly come to support, didn't.

Afterward, outside the venue, Abe found him leaning against a brick wall.

"You didn't feel it?"

Musa looked at him. Long.

"Was it for us... or for them?"

Abe blinked. "Can't it be both?"

"Not when sincerity is the currency."

Abe's jaw tightened. "I gave my heart."

"You gave your ego a mic."

That one hit hard. Abe turned away. Didn't respond. Musa didn't follow.

Back at the dorm, Tariq gathered the Circle—minus Musa, who hadn't answered his texts.

"I'm getting calls. Emails. Even a podcast invite."

Hasan raised an eyebrow. "A podcast?"

"Yep. Faith Unfiltered. Wants to do a feature."

Rohan asked, "Are we becoming influencers?"

Michael said, "No. But the world thinks we are."

Tariq sighed. "So how do we hold what we've built without selling it?"

Abe muttered, "Maybe we stop caring what other people think."

Rohan shot back, "That's how empires fall."

They all looked at each other. A little less unified. A little more real.

Tariq wrote that night:

> *It's easy to be honest when no one's listening. Harder when the room is full of people waiting to monetize your scars.*

A Crisis in the Quiet

Musa waited until after Maghrib. The lounge was half-lit. The air smelled faintly of jasmine tea and too many unanswered emails. Abe was scrolling, headphones in. Rohan scribbled on a legal pad. Tariq sat cross-legged, not reading, just holding a book open like a shield.

Musa stepped into the circle without ceremony. No greeting. No smile. Just: "I need to step back."

Abe looked up first. "What?"

"I need space," Musa said. "From the Circle. From the spotlight. From the noise."

Tariq's book closed slowly. Michael entered just in time to catch the sentence.

"Musa, is this about the comments? The mic night? The…"

"No," Musa said. "It's about me."

He sat down. Finally looked at all of them.

"I love what we've made. I believe in it. But I've been showing up empty. Spiritually. Emotionally. I've been praying out of memory, not meaning. And this thing we're building—it's beautiful, but it's not Allah."

Silence. Real. Heavy.

Then he added, quieter: "I think I started substituting brotherhood for worship. And I can't do that anymore."

Abe opened his mouth. Then closed it.

Tariq nodded slowly. Not with comfort. But with understanding he wished he didn't have to understand.

Later that night, Hasan received the formal email from the Dean's office. Subject: Academic Status Notification – Immediate Attention Required

It wasn't ambiguous. He was officially on probation. One more dropped grade, and he'd be suspended from the university.

He closed the email. Locked his laptop. And stared at the wall.

He didn't tell anyone. Not yet. Not because he was scared.

But because if he said it out loud, he feared the Circle would start treating him like glass. And he'd rather shatter quietly than be coddled while cracking.

Michael noticed it first. The way Hasan's notes stopped being organized. The way he stared longer at the same page. The way his tea stayed untouched.

Michael didn't ask. He just said, "Want to study together this week?"

Hasan blinked. Almost said no. Then nodded. "Yeah."

Michael smiled. "Good. I'll bring snacks."

Tariq stood in the hallway outside the lounge that night, texting Musa.

Tariq: "You still love us, right?"

Musa: "Of course. But I need to love Him more first."

Tariq didn't reply. He just stared at the words like scripture. Because maybe they were.

In the morning, Tariq sat alone in the masjid. No meeting. No speech. Just silence.

He didn't cry. Didn't journal. Just whispered: "Ya Allah, make the circle strong enough to still be whole when someone steps away."

Fault Lines

It started with a flyer. Again. Same red ink, same MSA bulletin board.

This one wasn't a critique. It was an announcement: "National Muslim Youth Leadership Summit" Hosted by Voices for Faith March 14–16, Washington, D.C. Keynote: Tariq Rahman?

The question mark was real. Because they hadn't confirmed it. But they had posted it.

Rohan was the first to find it. He took a photo. Sent it to the group chat.

Rohan: "You seeing this?"

Abe: "Let the man shine lol"

Michael: "Tariq... did you agree to this?"

Tariq: "No. I haven't responded yet."

Hasan: "Why not?"

Tariq: "Because I don't know what they're asking for. A voice? A face? A product?"

The chat went quiet. Then Abe replied—not in the chat, but in person.

He found Tariq near the halal cart on 116th.

"You know what your problem is?"

Tariq blinked. "You mean today?"

"You're scared of your own light. Scared that the second you speak too loud, you'll stop being sincere."

Tariq folded his arms. "You think I should just say yes to everything?"

"No. I think you should stop pretending you didn't ask for this."

Tariq stared at him. "Ask for what?"

"This," Abe gestured broadly. "All of it. The mic. The impact. The love. You didn't fall into leadership, bro. You stepped into it. Own it."

Tariq stepped back. "And what happens when it owns me?"

Abe didn't answer. Just shook his head and walked away.

That night, the Circle met in the dorm lounge.

Rohan brought a printed copy of the summit flyer. Placed it on the table.

Abe shrugged. "What's the big deal?"

Rohan leaned forward. "The big deal is we said we wouldn't turn this into a platform. We said it was sacred."

Abe shot back, "Sacred things don't die in sunlight."

Hasan whispered, "Some do."

Rohan stood. "Look, I love this brother. But if our circle becomes a stepping stone to someone's resume, we've already failed."

Tariq held up a hand.

"I haven't said yes."

"But you haven't said no," Rohan replied.

Michael cut in. "We're not voting on someone's integrity."

Abe folded his arms. "Feels like we are."

Silence.

Then Tariq said quietly: "I don't want to speak for us. I want to speak from us. But if that's not possible... I'll stay silent."

Later that night, Michael found Hasan in the stairwell. No reason. Just instinct. They sat. Quiet.

Then Michael asked, "You ever wonder if all of this is temporary?"

Hasan stared at the wall. "The Circle?"

"Everything. School. Identity. The comfort we pretend we earned."

Hasan didn't answer. Then he said:

"If I get suspended... I won't tell anyone until I'm already gone."

Michael looked at him. Long.

"You should let us carry you before you fall."

Hasan shook his head. "I was raised to carry others. Not the other way around."

Michael: "Yeah. Same. Look where it got us."

Tariq wrote that night:

> *I am not afraid of failure. I am afraid of becoming so polished*
> *they stop seeing the cracks I worked hard to live with.*

The Hinge

Friday night was supposed to be chill. Just dinner, maybe some tea. A few of them had floated the idea of catching a late film on campus. But when the emails kept buzzing, when the group chat filled with half-spoken frustrations and passive RSVPs, Tariq quietly changed the plan. "Let's just meet. One rug. No agenda."

No one objected. Not even Abe.

By 8:11 p.m., they were seated in a quiet corner of the campus musalla. Tariq brought a single lantern-style lamp.

Michael brought dates.

Rohan brought a printout of du'a for clarity.

Abe came empty-handed—but sat closer than usual.

Hasan looked exhausted.

Musa wasn't there.

No one mentioned it. But his absence was the room.

They prayed two rak'ahs. Not in jama'ah. Individually. Each of them with their own pace.

Tariq's was slow, barely moving. Abe rushed, but whispered every ayah with aching precision. Hasan stayed in sujood longer than he meant to. Michael forgot the second surah, but smiled anyway. Rohan cried in the second rak'ah—and didn't hide it.

Afterward, no one spoke for a while. The silence wasn't awkward. It was cleansing.

Then, quietly, Tariq opened his notebook and read: "I was asked to speak on behalf of Muslim youth in America. I said no."

Eyes lifted. He looked around. "Because I can't represent something I'm still becoming. And I won't turn the circle into a brand. This isn't a launchpad. It's a lifeline."

No claps. No praise. Just eye contact that felt like amens.

Rohan passed around cups of warm tea.

Abe finally said: "I've been showing off. And I've been hiding. At the same time."

Tariq: "Same."

Hasan said nothing. But his eyes welled.

Michael placed a hand on his shoulder. That was enough.

As they sat, the wind outside picked up. The musalla lights flickered once. And then steadied.

Tariq looked around. "We're not okay. Not fully. But we're still here."

They nodded. One by one. No need for ceremony. No need for resolve. Just presence. That was enough.

Later that night, Tariq sat on the rooftop. Sky dim with clouds.

He texted Musa.

Tariq: "We missed your presence tonight. But we carried your name in our prayer."

Musa: "That is enough. I'm still with you. Just walking slower now."

Tariq: "Slowness is a kind of prayer too."

He opened his journal. Wrote one line:

What we protect is more fragile now. But also more real.

CHAPTER ELEVEN

What Love Demands

When Silence Becomes Distance

The knock on Tariq's dorm door came just after Fajr.

Three firm taps. Not campus security. Not delivery. Not one of the brothers.

He opened it groggy, still blinking the last ayah of sujood out of his eyes.

His father stood in the doorway.

No warning. No "I'm in town."

Just a gray peacoat, leather gloves, and a face carved with the quiet discipline of a man who had never once asked for help.

"Tariq," he said. "Let's get breakfast."

They walked in silence to a small diner off Amsterdam Ave. Nothing fancy—just strong coffee and a laminated menu that hadn't changed since the 80s.

Tariq ordered tea. His father didn't. He just folded his hands.

And said: "So. Social work."

Tariq didn't answer. Because it wasn't a question. Just a loaded sentence dressed in casual tone.

"I got a message from Uncle Hanif," his father continued. "He said he saw something online. About a mic night. Something about healing. Poetry."

Tariq stirred his tea slowly. "We're doing something real," he said. "Not just creative. Transformative."

"And who asked you to transform anything?" his father said softly.

That stopped him cold.

"I thought you came to visit," Tariq said.

"I did," his father replied. "To see how far you've drifted."

The tea lost its flavor. The warmth of the room faded behind the fog of unspoken shame.

"I'm not ashamed," Tariq said, eyes locked.

"Then why didn't you tell us?" his father asked. "Why did I hear it from a WhatsApp uncle instead of my own son?"

Tariq looked down. Because he didn't know how to answer. Because deep down, he knew: He hadn't wanted to tell them. Not yet. Not until success softened the shock.

But his father wasn't angry. He was... quiet. Which was worse.

"I was proud," his father finally said, "when you got in. Columbia. Law track. The plan."

"I know."

"And now I don't know who you're becoming."

Tariq's voice cracked: "I'm still figuring that out."

"That's the part that scares me," his father whispered.

They didn't finish breakfast. Back on campus, Tariq didn't go to class. He walked the quad instead. Called Musa. No answer.

Texted Sonya.

Tariq: "You free later?"

No reply. Three hours passed. Then a text.

Sonya: "Not sure. Kinda in my own head right now."

He typed: "I get it. But I miss our honesty."

He watched the typing dots appear. Then vanish. She didn't respond again.

That night, Aisha passed Rohan in the med library.

He froze. She smiled. He nodded. She kept walking. But then turned.

"You okay?" she asked.

Rohan looked at her long.

Then said, "I'm fine."

But she didn't move. She just looked at him until he softened.

"I'm trying," he added.

Aisha nodded. "Trying is love too."

And she walked away.

In the dorm lounge, Abe played music under his breath.

Michael sat beside him, scrolling job listings he wasn't qualified for yet.

Hasan was... not present. Not just physically. Emotionally, he'd gone somewhere quiet, and none of them knew how to follow.

Tariq entered, hoodie up.

Eyes dull. No one spoke. They just let the silence hold them.

Because even silence, when shared, was a kind of reminder.

Later, in his journal, Tariq wrote:

> *My father wants certainty. Sonya wants distance. I want peace. But maybe peace isn't the absence of tension. Maybe it's the commitment to stay while the tension finds its name.*

Underneath the Versions

The Circle didn't meet in the lounge this time. They met in Room 406— Hasan's room. A place usually pristine: color-coded binders, stacked books by GPA relevance, incense trays with exact burn times.

But tonight, it was dim. One overhead light. Clutter on the desk. Hasan didn't say much. He just opened the door and said: "Come in if you want. Don't knock. Don't ask."

They all came. Michael first, holding a thermos of chai. Then Rohan, no laptop for once. Abe entered with his hoodie over his head like he wasn't ready to speak. Tariq brought nothing but his presence.

Hasan sat on the edge of his bed. Spoke without looking up. "I got the letter two weeks ago."

No one asked what letter. They knew.

He continued: "Academic probation. Official. Not a warning. A countdown."

The air in the room froze. Abe exhaled. Michael looked down. Hasan still didn't meet anyone's eyes.

"I've spent three years being the responsible one. The spreadsheet guy. The one who never forgets group deadlines. The one whose calendar sends reminders to everyone else."

His voice cracked. "And I've failed every midterm this semester."

Still, no one spoke. So he kept going.

"I've been living underneath the version of me that everyone expects. The one my parents brags about in masjid lobbies. The one who's supposed to be the future of our family's real estate empire. The one who—"

He stopped. Looked up. Eyes wet. "The one who's not allowed to be weak."

Michael moved first. No words. Just stood. Walked to the bookshelf. Took the topmost binder—labeled "Fall Semester Strategy"—and closed it gently. Then turned to Hasan and said: "You don't owe us perfection. You owe us presence."

Hasan wiped his face. Didn't cry. But breathed. For the first time in weeks, he breathed.

Rohan, uncharacteristically still, leaned back. Spoke low: "My family thinks I'll take over the mango business by 26. They don't know I can't even finish a business ethics paper without breaking out in hives."

Abe laughed quietly. "Yo, I've been telling people I'm applying to grad school. I'm not. I'm scared of more school. I'm scared I peaked in the Circle."

Tariq whispered: "I haven't told my parents I changed my major. They still think I'm on the law track."

Michael added, "My parents don't even know I applied to internships outside tech. I told them it was for a coding boot camp."

The room was heavy. Not with shame. But truth. Shared like oxygen. Passed around like survival.

Hasan finally looked at Tariq.

"What happens when we stop being who we're expected to be?"

Tariq met his gaze.

"We lose the audience. But we find each other."

They prayed 'Isha together that night. Slow. Soft. No leader announced. Just someone starting—and the rest following with unspoken permission.

Afterward, they sat in a circle on the carpet. No agenda. No flyer. Just five young men who'd just taken off their masks, even if just for an hour. And that was enough.

In his journal later, Tariq wrote:

> *There are versions of me still living in other people's minds. But tonight I watched them die. And I didn't mourn. I just… breathed.*

The Shape of Distance

Tariq saw Sonya near the Low Library steps, where the breeze always felt sharper, and the light hit the marble-like memory. She was standing alone, scrolling her phone, headphones in.

He hesitated. Then walked toward her. She looked up. Didn't smile. Didn't frown. Just removed one earbud and said, "Hey." It was soft. Not awkward. Just… worn.

"Hey," he replied. "Can we talk?" She nodded and led him toward a quieter bench near the statue of Alma Mater.

They sat. Distance between them wide enough to hold the tension.

He started. "I know you've been quiet."

She tilted her head. "So have you."

"Yeah," he said. "I guess I didn't know how to ask if we were okay without making it sound like I wanted more than we agreed on."

She laughed. Once. "No one agreed on anything, Tariq. That's the problem."

He looked down. "I miss the honesty," he said.

"I miss the ease," she replied.

That hit harder than he expected.

"I don't know when things got complicated," he whispered.

"Probably around the time we started pretending this was just friendship."

He didn't respond. Not right away. Then:

"What if I'm not ready to lose what we are... even if I don't know what it is?"

Sonya looked at him long. Then said: "Then let's stop trying to name it. Let's just protect it. Whatever it is."

He nodded. And they sat. Not holding hands. Not trading promises. Just breathing in a closeness that no longer demanded definition.

Elsewhere on campus, Rohan stood outside the pharmacy building, debating whether to text Aisha. He already had the message typed: "I don't have the right words. But I'd like to try being honest. With you. No pressure."

He stared at it. Then hit send.

Waited. Watched the dots appear. Then vanish. Then appear again.

Aisha: "Honesty is a start. I'm listening."

He exhaled so deeply that he almost fell forward.

Back in the dorm lounge, Abe was making moves. Alone. On his laptop, designing a new flyer: "Healing Spaces: A Night of Unfiltered Muslim Creativity" Presented by The Circle (No RSVP Needed. No Judgment Allowed.)

He didn't ask the others. Didn't post it. Yet. But the Canva draft was saved. And the date—next Friday—was circled in his planner.

He was planning it fast, excited. Maybe too fast. Maybe not out of vision. But out of fear. That the fire was dying. And he needed to spark something before it got quiet again.

Tariq returned to the dorm later. Didn't tell the brothers about Sonya. Didn't talk about silence. He just walked in and said: "I think sometimes love is not asking someone to stay, but giving them the space to return."

No one questioned it. Michael just nodded. Hasan looked away. Rohan smiled—barely. Abe didn't hear him. He was still editing the flyer.

In his journal, Tariq wrote:

> *She didn't leave. She just let the silence speak first. And I finally listened.*

A Gathering Without Permission

Abe didn't tell anyone. Not because he was trying to be secretive. But because he was convinced he was being efficient.

The first email went out Tuesday morning: "A night of Muslim creativity. Stories. Rhymes. Truth. No filter. No flyers on approval. Just faith and fire." He signed it: The Circle.

By noon, RSVPs were trickling in.

By 4 p.m., his Instagram story was flooded with reposts.

By midnight, people were asking if it was "the sequel to *Not Perfect, Just Honest.*"

Abe smiled. That was the point. Except this time, the Circle wasn't involved. Not really.

He didn't mean to bypass them. He just... didn't want to ask for permission to move the spirit.

Tariq noticed the shift first. Not in words. In vibe.

When Abe entered the lounge, his energy was up—hype, magnetic, just a little too polished. His eyes darted more. His hoodie looked ironed.

And when Hasan asked what he was working on, Abe just grinned and said, "Something big. Y'all'll see."

That night, Rohan pulled Michael aside. "You feel that?"

Michael nodded. "Something's cooking. But no one's stirring it together."

Hasan was too busy to care. He'd locked himself in the campus library with a wall of textbooks and a plastic bag full of halal takeout. He hadn't responded to Circle messages in three days.

Tariq checked on him once, got a thumbs-up through the glass. Didn't push. But it felt like retreat. Not out of ego. Out of self-preservation.

Meanwhile, Musa reappeared. Not in person. In an email.

> *Subject: Du'a Request + Salaam*
>
> *To: The Circle*
>
> *From: Musa.Diallo@columbia.edu*
>
> *Time: 3:11 a.m.*
>
> **Assalaamu Alaikum wa Rahmatullah, brothers—*
>
> *I'm still walking slow. Still praying alone. Still trying to remember what presence without noise looks like. But I heard about the mic night follow-up. Heard our name was used. I'm not upset. Just... uneasy. We made something with intention. Let's not turn it into a tour. Pray for me. I'll return soon. Maybe not to the room, but always to the bond.*
>
> *Was-salaam,*
>
> *Musa**

Tariq read it three times. Then closed his laptop. Not with anger. But with a heavy knowing: They were drifting.

Not from betrayal. But from lack of alignment.

Back in the dorm, Abe finalized his venue. A reclaimed art space in Harlem. No permissions needed. Just a deposit and a fire extinguisher.

He was proud.

He posted another teaser flyer. This time, he tagged the Circle.

Tariq saw it. Messaged him directly.

Tariq: "Bro. You tagged the Circle. But we haven't even talked."

Abe: "Didn't think we had to. The spirit's the same. Right?"

Tariq: "Intention isn't inherited. It's rebuilt every time."

No reply.

That night, Michael visited Tariq's room. Held up his phone. "Want to see something?"

It was a group message Abe had posted in a different student org chat: "Circle 2.0 coming soon. Less rules. More fire. Let's make history again."

Michael looked up.

"He's not trying to hurt us," he said.

Tariq nodded.

"But that doesn't mean we won't bleed."

In his journal that night, Tariq wrote:

> *Sometimes betrayal wears a smile. Sometimes ambition forgets its wudu. And sometimes, love means naming the drift before it becomes distance.*

What Love Really Costs

It wasn't planned. The confrontation. But real love rarely is. It happened on Thursday night, the day before Abe's solo event. The Circle gathered in the lounge—not for prayer, not for strategy. For clarity.

Tariq had called it. Michael had seconded. Rohan showed up first, already tense. Hasan arrived with his laptop, eyes sunken, ready to leave if it turned into drama. Abe walked in last—hood up, earbuds out, bounce in his step like he wasn't walking into fire.

Tariq didn't waste time. "Why didn't you tell us?"

Abe dropped onto the arm of the couch with an exaggerated sigh. "Man, y'all acting like I hijacked the ummah. It's just an event."

"But it's under our name," Rohan said. "With no discussion. That's not just an event. That's co-opting something sacred."

Abe's jaw tightened. "You think I don't care about the Circle?"

"No," Michael said gently. "We think you care too much about what it gives you."

That stopped him.

Tariq leaned forward. "You wanted to keep the fire going. I get it. We all feel it fading sometimes. But Abe... we don't spark fire by pretending it's still lit. We spark it by tending the embers."

Abe stood now. "I made this. I helped make this. And now I feel like I need permission to breathe?"

"You need accountability," Rohan said.

Abe looked at him. "From who? You? Mr. PowerPoint Prophet? You want to schedule my sincerity too?"

That one hit sharp.

Rohan looked away.

Tariq stood. "This isn't about control, Abe. It's about covenant. We said we'd build something together. And that means none of us gets to solo in a space meant for circle."

Silence. The room pulsed.

Abe finally spoke—softer now. "I'm scared, man. Scared we're losing it. The meaning. The impact. The identity. I don't want to fade into a group chat of what used to be."

Tariq's voice dropped. "Then say that. Don't call it vision when it's fear. Don't put our name on something we didn't shape together."

The door opened. They all turned.

Musa. No backpack. No shoes. Just socks and a tasbih looped around his wrist. "Is this a closed meeting?" he asked softly.

"No," Michael said. "It's a Circle."

Musa nodded. Entered. Sat on the floor.

Tariq looked at him. "How'd you know to come?"

Musa smiled. "I prayed. And the prayer walked me here."

Abe sat too. Tension leaking out of him slowly. "I thought I was honoring the work," he whispered.

"You were," Musa replied. "But the work doesn't live in events. It lives in submission."

Abe exhaled. "So what now?"

Michael: "We rebuild trust."

Rohan: "We pause the event."

Hasan: "We take care of each other before we take care of impact."

Tariq: "We remind the world that what we made wasn't content. It was covenant."

Musa nodded. "Then let's make du'a together."

They turned the lights down. Made wudu in silence. Prayed two rak'ahs. No speeches. No closure. Just a room of young men learning how to hold what love really costs.

Later that night, Abe deleted the flyer. Posted a final story: "Sometimes the most honest thing you can do is not perform. Tonight, I remember why we started. The Circle is still intact. Alhamdulillah."

Tariq sat on the rooftop again. The city below didn't know what had just been saved. But he did.

He wrote:

Love without boundaries becomes burden. And brotherhood without accountability becomes noise. Tonight we chose quiet. And quiet carried us back to truth.

CHAPTER TWELVE

The Choice to Stay

When the Letter Comes

The letter arrived on a Wednesday. A manila envelope, hand-delivered to the dorm's mailroom. Thick paper. No fanfare.

Hasan didn't open it right away. He placed it on his desk like it might explode. Went to class. Came back. Ate half a falafel wrap. Cleaned his desk twice.

Read one page of a textbook he didn't understand. Prayed *Dhuhr* in a whisper. Then sat down. And opened it.

> *Dear Mr. Rahman,*
>
> *We regret to inform you that due to ongoing academic performance concerns and a failure to meet the probationary GPA threshold as outlined in your prior notification, you will be required to take a mandatory leave of absence for the upcoming semester.*
>
> *You may reapply for reinstatement following the completion of summer coursework and with appropriate documentation of academic readiness. Please consult with your assigned dean and financial aid representative for transition support.*
>
> *We recognize the challenges of maintaining rigorous academic standards, and we encourage you to reflect, recalibrate, and*

return stronger.

Sincerely,

Office of Undergraduate Academic Affairs

Hasan read it once. Then again. Then set it down. Folded his hands. And said, softly: "It's done."

He didn't cry. Didn't punch anything. Didn't call home. He just stared at the window until the sun moved an inch, and the world looked slightly different— like the air had exhaled without him.

He didn't know what to feel. Just that something had ended. Not permanently. But deeply.

The Circle met that evening, just after Maghrib. Only four of them: Tariq. Rohan. Michael. Abe.

Musa had texted in: "With family tonight. Make du'a."

Hasan arrived last. Bag heavy. Eyes tired. He sat, pulled the letter from his coat pocket, and handed it to Tariq without a word.

Tariq read it slowly. Twice. Then passed it to Michael.

No one reacted right away.

Abe broke the silence. "We're not gonna let them kick you out like that, man."

Hasan raised an eyebrow. "They're not kicking me out. They're giving me a semester to remember who I am."

Michael asked, "Are you okay?"

"I don't know."

Tariq leaned forward. "Do you want to stay? Or is this... a needed pause?"

Hasan looked around. Then said, quiet and plain: "I want to stay. But my mind isn't. My body's here. My spirit's somewhere in the Bronx, trying to help my mom figure out why the mortgage company keeps calling."

Pause.

"My little sister's about to graduate high school. No college fund. No plan. And I'm over here trying to explain to professors why I can't finish a group project."

He looked down.

"So maybe this is Allah's way of giving me a break... before I break."

No one argued. Because nothing they could say would fix it.

Instead, Michael pulled a notebook from his backpack. Tore out a page. Wrote his number, email, home address. Pushed it across the table.

"So you have it. For whenever."

Rohan followed.

Then Tariq.

Then Abe, who included a hand-drawn map to the *halal* burger spot they always joked about taking a road trip to.

Hasan smiled. Barely. But it was real.

They prayed together that night. All five of them. In the dorm lounge.

Lights dim. Hearts heavy.

Hasan led. Not because he asked. Because he needed to. His voice cracked in *sujood*. But he never stopped.

Afterward, no one moved.

Abe finally said: "I love you, bro."

Hasan replied: "Y'all are the reason I made it this far."

Back in his room, Hasan wrote his first journal entry in months:

Sometimes leaving isn't failure. Sometimes it's faith in disguise. I'm not done. Just... detouring through survival.

At the same time, Tariq got another email. Subject: "Keynote Opportunity – Muslim Youth Now: Elevating the Next Generation"

From a well-known national nonprofit. The same organization that once ignored his emails. Now asking him to headline their annual summit.

All expenses paid. Video spotlight. National stream.

He read it once. Then again. Then closed his laptop.

And whispered: "Why now?"

In his journal, he wrote:

> *They call when you're visible. But they never ask how much you've lost in the light. I don't know if I want the mic. I just want my brother to stay.*

Breaking the News

Hasan sat in the stairwell of the student union building. Fourth floor. No traffic. No echoes. Just quiet enough to hear his own breath—and the distant thrum of a vending machine that hadn't worked since orientation.

His phone was in his lap. Dialed. Not yet calling.

He had rehearsed the conversation a dozen times. But nothing he practiced sounded like love.

Or strength.

Only failure.

Finally, he pressed Call. His mother answered on the third ring.

"Assalaamu Alaikum, beta."

He smiled despite himself.

"Wa Alaikum Salaam, Ma."

"You okay?"

"Yeah."

Pause.

"No."

She inhaled. Deep. Slow.

The kind of breath only mothers take when they already know something's wrong.

"Say it."

So he did. He told her about the grades. The letter. The leave of absence. The reapplication process. The probable loss of some scholarship money.

The shame.

The guilt.

The silence he had worn like armor.

She didn't interrupt. Not once.

When he finished, she asked only one thing:

"Are you safe?"

He blinked.

"What?"

"Are you safe? Are you eating? Sleeping? Breathing without a rock on your chest?"

His voice cracked.

"Barely."

Her voice was soft. "Then come home. And let's fix the rest together."

Hasan cried like he hadn't since childhood.

Not loud. Not desperate. But fully. The kind of crying that clears space inside the ribs.

Later, in the lounge, the brothers were packing a small box for him—books, snacks, notebooks.

Abe added a du'a card and a mini LED prayer lamp.

Michael handed him a thumb drive labeled: "Survival Kit: Playlists + Quran Recitations + Memes."

Rohan added a copy of The Alchemist, marked with sticky notes on pages he thought "felt right."

Tariq brought nothing but an envelope. Inside: a letter. Not typed. Not signed. Just written in blue ink:

"When the road curves, it doesn't mean the destination moved.

You're still on the path.

We'll be right behind you—every step.

One ummah. One circle. One you."

Hasan tucked it into his coat pocket. Didn't read it again. Didn't need to.

The night before he left, they prayed together one last time.

Just the five of them. No photos. No tears. Just long sajdah and a whispered Ameen that felt like both a goodbye and a promise.

Tariq stayed behind after everyone left. Sat in the dark lounge. Reopened the email from the nonprofit: We'd be honored to feature your voice as the future of Muslim leadership. Let us know by Friday. We'll arrange your flight and housing."

He stared at it. Then typed a reply. Deleted it. Typed again.

Paused.

At that exact moment, his phone buzzed.

Text from Hasan: "Say yes if you need to. But only if it feeds your soul—not your followers."

Tariq stared at the screen. Smiled. Closed his laptop.

And said softly: "BarakAllahu feek, brother."

In his journal, he wrote:

> *We said goodbye without breaking. That means we were built on something real. Some people stay by presence. Others by prayer. Either way—we're still held.*

Permission to Lead

Tariq sat at the edge of the reflecting pool on campus. The sky was grey. Cold but not cruel.

It had been three days since Hasan left. Three days since the email invite sat unanswered in his inbox.

He'd read it over and over. Every sentence buzzed with opportunity—and expectation.

"We believe your voice is essential in shaping the next era of American Muslim leadership..."

"Your story reflects the lived experience of thousands of students navigating identity, faith, and service..."

"Our audience needs inspiration. Our community needs you."

It didn't feel like a compliment. It felt like a crown. And he wasn't sure he wanted it. He met with each of the brothers, one at a time.

Michael first.

They sat on the campus mosque steps. Michael passed him a cup of hot chocolate from the vending machine that never made it right.

"It's okay to lead," Michael said. "Just don't let them define what that means."

Tariq nodded. "What if I don't know what it means yet?"

Michael smiled. "Then lead by learning out loud."

Rohan met him at the library.

They didn't talk for the first ten minutes. Then Rohan looked up from his notes and said: "You're not a spokesperson. You're a signal."

"What's that supposed to mean?"

Rohan shrugged. "People don't need you to say it perfectly. They need to know someone is saying it—and trying to live it."

Abe surprised him.

They bumped into each other near the smoothie bar. Tariq was about to dodge the topic. But Abe beat him to it.

"Bro," he said, "If I were you, I'd say yes."

Tariq blinked. "Really?"

"Yeah. But only after you ask yourself one thing."

"What?"

"If no one clapped—would you still say it?"

Tariq didn't answer. Not right away.

Later that night, he called Musa.

They hadn't spoken in over a week—just a few short texts.

Musa picked up on the second ring.

"Salaam, brother."

"Wa alaikum salaam."

They sat in silence for a moment—familiar, unforced.

Tariq finally said, "I got asked to speak. Big stage. Muslim youth summit. All the buzzwords."

Musa chuckled. "And you want permission?"

Tariq exhaled. "Yeah. Maybe."

Musa's voice was soft. "Then I give you none."

Tariq froze.

But Musa continued. "Because you don't need permission. You need intention. If your niyyah is clean—speak. If it's clouded—wait. But don't ask men to give you what only Allah can approve."

Tariq nodded slowly. "And if I say yes?"

"Then speak like you're still praying," Musa said. "Not like you're performing."

That night, Tariq opened his laptop. Clicked Reply.

Typed one sentence: I will speak, in sha Allah—so long as I'm not expected to be perfect, only present.

He hit send. Then prayed two rak'ahs. Not for approval. For sincerity.

In his journal, he wrote:

> *Leadership isn't the mic. It's the mirror. And today, for the first time, I didn't flinch when I looked into it.*

In the Absence

The difference wasn't loud. No chairs missing. No speeches unspoken. No blowouts.

Just... a shift. Small things. Like the group messages feeling thinner. Like the snack shelf in the lounge going stale—no one buying the spicy almonds Hasan liked. Like the way the brothers now paused when it was time to start prayer, unsure who should lead.

Before, it had been obvious. Now, it wasn't.

Michael noticed first. He arrived early to their Thursday night check-in. Alone. Turned on the lights. The hum of the room felt wrong. Too quiet. He pulled out his notebook.

Opened to a page labeled "Circle 2024 Vision." And stared at it.

Nothing he had planned felt relevant anymore. Without Hasan, the rhythm was off. He was the one who tracked the timelines. Managed the flyers. Organized the prayer rotations. He wasn't the center— but he'd been the clock. And now the time felt broken.

Abe entered ten minutes late. No apology. Just loud energy and a new idea: "Yo. I got an offer from the campus diversity center to run a spoken word workshop next month. I said I'd do it under the Circle's name."

Michael blinked. "You said that without asking?"

Abe shrugged. "They asked last minute. I figured we'd all be down. It's the mission, right?"

Michael paused. "That's not the point. It's the process."

"Since when did you become the gatekeeper?" Abe snapped.

Michael looked up, surprised by the heat.

Rohan entered mid-sentence. "Did I miss something?"

Abe dropped into a chair, crossing his arms. "Apparently, I'm not allowed to move the mission forward unless I check in first."

Rohan raised his hands. "Okay. Let's breathe. What's happening here?"

Michael turned to him. "We used to move like a circle. Now it's starting to feel like a brand."

Abe shot back. "That's because some of us think this is seminary when the world is asking for a movement."

The room went still. Tariq entered late. Caught the tension instantly. Paused. Looked at all of them.

"Where's the barakah?"

That quieted everything. He walked to the whiteboard. Erased the old list of next steps. Wrote one sentence in its place: Are we still a circle?

Then he sat.

Michael spoke first. "I feel like I'm planning in a vacuum. No flow. No structure."

Rohan added: "We've lost our rhythm."

Abe didn't speak. Just bounced his leg.

Tariq looked at him.

"Abe. Talk to us."

Silence. Then finally: "I'm scared we're losing relevance. That we'll fade into another MSA spinoff with no spine."

Tariq nodded. "And what if we do?"

Abe blinked. "What?"

"What if we fade? What if this isn't forever? What if it was just meant to be what it was?"

That quieted the room again.

Michael spoke: "Then let's go out with integrity. Not inflation."

Rohan: "Or maybe... we evolve."

Tariq exhaled. Then stood. "But if we keep calling this a circle, we have to move like one."

That night, Musa texted the group chat: "Missed prayer with y'all today. But I made du'a at maghrib: that Allah keeps our hearts soft. Not just loud."

No one replied right away. But they all read it. Twice.

Tariq sat in the masjid after Isha, alone.

Wrote in his journal:

> *Absence creates questions. Not all of them have answers. But if we can survive silence— maybe the circle is real after all.*

A Letter from Hasan

It came on a Sunday. No warning. Just an envelope slid under the dorm lounge door in the middle of the afternoon.

Handwritten. To: The Circle, From: H.R., Return address: Bronx, NY

Michael found it first. Held it like something holy. Didn't open it. Waited until they were all there—Tariq, Abe, Rohan, and him.

They sat in a loose square on the floor, backs against chairs, feet tangled in stray cords and prayer beads.

Then Michael read it aloud.

Bismillah...

My brothers,

I've rewritten this letter four times. Once angry. Once sad. Once trying to sound strong. Once trying to sound fine. But the truth is, I'm all of those things.

Being away from campus is strange. The noise is gone. The pressure too.

But so is the comfort. So is the Circle. I miss you. But I'm also healing.

I didn't realize how much I had broken until Allah gave me the quiet to listen to my soul again. I've been praying on the roof of our building. Reading Qur'an out loud for no one but myself. And helping my mom sleep without having to worry about bills.

That alone is a kind of ibadah I never respected until now.

I've had to mourn who I thought I'd be by this point. A future valedictorian. A planner. A perfectionist with a polished five-year plan. That's gone. And alhamdulillah for it.

Because what I'm building now isn't for a resume. It's for Jannah.

I don't know if I'll be back next semester. That's in Allah's hands. But I do know this: You all changed me. In ways I didn't know I needed. You showed me that masculinity doesn't have to mean silence. That Islam doesn't have to feel like a burden. That brotherhood isn't a side quest—it's the backbone.

So if the Circle goes on without me—good. Let it evolve. Let it break and rebuild. Let it be tested. But never forget what it was born from: breath, not applause.

If you remember nothing else I've said, remember this: We were real. And we were enough.

Du'a always,

–Hasan

When the reading ended, no one moved. Michael folded the letter neatly. Placed it on the table.

Tariq wiped his eyes.

Abe stared at the floor.

Rohan whispered: "SubhanAllah."

Then Michael stood. "Let's pray."

And they did. Together. Still four bodies. But never less than a Circle.

Tariq journaled that night:

We didn't lose Hasan. We made room for his return—in whatever form it takes. That's love. That's Islam. That's the Circle.

Chapter Thirteen

The Next Flame

The Invitation

The email didn't come through Tariq. It came through Michael. Which made it feel different from the start. The subject line read: "Formal Invitation – Unified Muslim Youth Coalition (UMYC): Spring Convening"

Michael opened it without fanfare. Read the first two lines. Then the next five. Then the attached PDF. Then sat back in his chair and stared at the ceiling.

This wasn't just another open mic invite. It was infrastructure. Money. Press. Movement builders. Panelists from all five boroughs. A 200-person summit scheduled for Ramadan weekend. And they wanted the Circle on stage. Not just present. Featured.

Michael shared the email in the group thread with a single message:

Michael: "We need to talk. This is... big."

They met that night in the lounge. Five strong again—Musa had returned quietly, without speech. He brought mango juice and seated himself cross-legged like nothing had ever changed. The email was projected onto the whiteboard. No one touched their phones.

Tariq read aloud:

The Unified Muslim Youth Coalition (UMYC) would be

honored to feature The Circle in our opening program. Your voices represent an authentic, necessary pulse in the modern Muslim youth experience…

…We are particularly interested in your spiritual honesty, racial diversity, and ability to speak across boundaries without compromising religious identity…

…We are offering each invited organization a $3,000 stipend, along with national exposure, strategic mentorship opportunities, and access to a broader network of Muslim professionals and activists…

Please confirm participation by this Friday.

Silence.

Then Abe: "They said 'stipend,' right? That's not a typo?"

Michael: "Three stacks. Real."

Rohan: "And a livestream."

Musa said nothing. Just tapped his misbaha slowly.

Tariq looked around. "So what are we thinking?"

Michael went first. "It's huge. But also risky. I don't know who these people are yet. We're not a brand—they keep treating us like one."

Rohan: "But this is how legacy starts. You don't scale by staying silent."

Abe: "It's the next logical move. But I'm not interested in being someone's 'faith-flavored content strategy.'"

Tariq: "What would saying yes mean?"

Musa finally spoke. His voice was calm. Precise. "It would mean stepping into a space that expects you to lead. And possibly—to sell."

Tariq met his eyes. "And if we don't go?"

Musa didn't blink. "Then we keep building with our own hands. Quietly. Slowly. With sincerity instead of reach."

Another pause.

Then Abe laughed. "Man, you talk like a monk."

Musa smirked. "Or maybe just like a man who's watched sincerity bleed under bright lights."

Later, after the meeting dispersed, Michael lingered with Tariq. They walked the edge of campus under low streetlamps.

"You want to do it?" Michael asked.

Tariq shrugged. "I want to say something real. But I'm tired of being the face of what we haven't all agreed to carry."

Michael nodded "Then don't speak for us. Speak from us."

That sat deep.

That night, Tariq journaled:

> *The mic keeps coming back. The stage keeps widening. The invitations keep sounding like praise—but underneath, I hear contracts. We can show up. But only if we arrive as servants, not stars.*

The Fire We Chose

They met again the next night—same room, different tension.

This time, no laptops. Just five brothers and one question: "Do we go?"

Not *can we.*

Not *should we.*

Do we?

Rohan was first to speak. He stood near the window, arms crossed.

"Look, I'm not saying we sell out. But this is infrastructure. Money, connections, legit movement-building. If we keep hiding from opportunity, we'll stay small forever."

Michael countered. "It's not hiding. It's discerning. Who funds this? Who runs it? What do they expect us to say—or not say?"

Abe chimed in, leaning back in his chair, legs stretched. "Yo, they're offering money and a platform. That's not evil. That's logistics."

Musa stirred his tea. Quietly. Then said: "The first time I ever joined a coalition, I was 16."

Everyone turned. Musa didn't look up. "West African youth network. Back home. They recruited me because I was a *hafiz*.

Put me on flyers. Pushed me to speak at rallies. I was their 'spiritual backbone.' Their moral window dressing."

Abe whistled under his breath.

Musa continued. "It felt good. The attention. The applause. The way adults shook my hand after every talk like I was already something more than a teenager with memorized Arabic and no clue what to do with it."

He looked up. "And then one day, a speaker got up and said something I couldn't *cosign*. About gender. About Islam. It wasn't my lane. But my name was on the brochure. My silence became consent."

Silence.

"That was the day I realized: You don't need a mic to say something. You just need to stand on the wrong stage."

Tariq nodded slowly. The room sat heavy in it

Then he said: "What if we set terms?"

Rohan raised an eyebrow. "Terms?"

"We go. But on our principles. We define what we say. What we don't. What we won't compromise."

Michael leaned in. "And if they push back?"

Tariq: "Then we walk."

Musa: "You're not afraid they'll replace us with louder voices?"

Tariq smiled. "Maybe they should. Noise is easy to find. Presence takes patience."

Abe tapped his chest once, then spoke. "I'll be real. I want the mic. I want the room. I want people to know we built something that wasn't perfect, but was honest. I'm not scared of attention. I'm scared of being forgotten."

Musa: "Then don't perform. Just tell the truth. If that's what they forget, then they weren't your people anyway."

They agreed that night to draft their terms. A list of non-negotiables. No filters. No censorship. No tokenism. If the coalition accepted—they'd go. If not—they'd stay behind. Together.

After the meeting, Tariq walked with Musa across campus. The wind had picked up. Students walked past them, laughing, phone lights blinking, doors slamming open and closed behind them like a world that never paused.

Musa said: "You're becoming a leader, you know."

Tariq shrugged. "I didn't ask to be."

Musa smiled. "That's usually how it works."

Later, in his journal, Tariq wrote:

> *We chose fire once. Not because we wanted to burn. But because we needed heat to shape something real. Now they're offering us a torch. But we'll only carry it if we can still walk barefoot.*

The Terms We Name

They met in Michael's room to draft the letter. Not in the lounge. Not in the masjid. Somewhere quieter. Somewhere more contained.

Tariq sat at the desk, fingers poised over the keyboard. Rohan had pulled out a notepad.

Abe was pacing.

Michael leaned against the dresser, arms folded.

Musa sat on the floor, back against the bed, beads clicking rhythmically in his fingers like punctuation marks.

"Let's be clear," Tariq said. "This isn't a list of demands. It's a statement of identity."

Abe nodded. "But still firm."

Michael: "Not arrogant. Just anchored."

Musa: "Not trying to lead everyone. Just refusing to lie."

They started slow. Line by line. The non-negotiables:

We speak freely and with integrity—without censorship or language constraints.

Our presence is collaborative, not symbolic. We will not serve as diversity decoration.

Our language will include faith references—Qur'an, du'a, Arabic terms—and we will not dilute them for mainstream comfort.

We are not influencers. We do not sell our brotherhood. We offer it in truth, not in performance.

We ask that the space respect prayer times and allow for communal salah.

No performance time limits for our segment unless all others are bound equally.

We reserve the right to walk away from the stage at any point if the core values of the Circle are compromised.

When they finished, they reread it three times. Each word felt inspirational.

Musa looked up. "What we've written is not a letter. It's a mirror."

Tariq hit "Send."

Two days passed. The response came on a Friday afternoon. Subject: "Re: Circle Participation – Adjustments Needed"

Michael opened it. Then forwarded it to the group thread. Then walked out of the library to breathe.

They met in the lounge. Again. Lights low. Hearts uncertain.

Tariq read aloud:

"Thank you for your thoughtful submission. We are deeply moved by your clarity of intention and passion for authentic community work..."

"...While we honor your integrity, we would like to offer the following adjustments in the spirit of logistical balance and cohesion across the event's programming..."

Then came the list:

- Replace "Islamic phrases" with English translations for accessibility
- Limit speaking time to five minutes
- Remove the clause about walking away from the stage
- Approve any statements referencing Palestine, gender identity, or political issues with organizers ahead of time
- Keep post-talk Q&A questions pre-screened to avoid audience disruption

Tariq finished reading. Closed the email. No one spoke.

Rohan was first to break the silence. "This isn't just edits. This is erosion."

Michael: "They want our voice. Not our conviction."

Abe ran a hand through his hair. "We could edit. Compromise. Say 70% of what we mean. That's still... something, right?"

Musa looked directly at him. "Something broken."

Tariq stood. "If we agree to this, we teach the next ones coming up that truth needs translation to be tolerable."

Michael: "So we walk?"

Rohan: "It might be our most important walk yet."

They sat down together. Reopened the draft. Typed their reply:

Thank you for your response. We humbly decline participation under the adjusted terms.

We pray your event succeeds in bringing light and sincerity to our communities.

May Allah grant barakah to your work.

They signed it: The Circle

Later that night, they gathered for prayer.

Musa led. Tariq made the intention. They didn't mention the event again. But their posture in prayer said everything: We did not shrink. We did not sell. We did not lie.

Tariq's journal that night:

> *Sometimes the world offers you a mic, but only if you whisper what they wrote for you. Tonight, we turned down the mic. And heard our souls again.*

A New Spark

It started with a knock. Not at the lounge door. Not a campus email.

Just a knock—at the stairwell wall where the Circle often prayed late at night.

Three students stood outside. Freshmen. Two brothers. One sister. Nervous. Hopeful.

One of them—Amira—clutched a printed flyer from the original open mic.

The one with the chalkboard. The candle. The quote: "Not Perfect. Just Honest."

The other two—Kareem and Jawad—looked like they had rehearsed what they wanted to say and were still terrified they'd forget it.

Tariq opened the door.

"Can we help you?"

Amira smiled. "We want to build something. And we don't want to do it alone."

They sat together in the back of the lounge. No one else from the Circle was there yet. Tariq listened as they spoke. About how the open mic changed the way they saw themselves. About how they hadn't felt welcome in masjid youth spaces. Too strict. Too filtered. Too cold. About how they wanted to plan a weekend retreat for Muslim students in the city. No institutions. No hierarchy. Just honesty, prayer, rest, and rebuilding.

"We were wondering..." Jawad added, voice shaking a little, "...if the Circle would help us anchor it."

Tariq didn't answer right away. Because what they were asking wasn't logistical. It was spiritual permission.

He told them he'd bring it to the brothers. He promised nothing.

But in his chest, a small ember caught fire The Circle met that night.

Musa looked tired but present.

Abe was uncharacteristically quiet.

Rohan had come straight from office hours and was still holding a half-graded econ quiz.

Michael just said what everyone else was thinking: "Are we even in a place to lead?"

Tariq replied: "Maybe leadership isn't about being ahead. Maybe it's about standing still long enough for someone else to find you."

Abe finally spoke. "I'm not perfect. I still feel the pull for shine. For platforms. For being seen." He looked up. "But helping them... it doesn't feel like ego. It feels like service."

Musa nodded. "Then it's worth doing."

They made a decision. No flyers. No PR. No branding. Just presence.

The Circle would co-organize. They'd mentor, not manage. Support, not spotlight. And whatever came of it, it would be purely theirs.

Later that night, Tariq journaled:

> *Maybe we were never meant to be a movement. Maybe we were just the soil. And now it's time for someone else to grow.*

Light in the Woods

They didn't rent a luxury cabin. No retreat center. No welcome packets.

Just two vans, fifteen Muslim students, a portable prayer mat, and a campground in upstate New York that didn't ask questions and charged half-price for student groups.

Tariq sat in the front seat of the second van, watching trees blur past as the city faded in the mirrors.

Michael drove.

Abe DJ'd off a cracked speaker.

In the rearview, Musa was teaching Kareem how to tie his prayer cap properly.

Amira was writing something in a spiral notebook, knees hugged to her chest.

Tariq just watched. And breathed.

The retreat wasn't flawless. They forgot the firewood. Someone brought haram marshmallows. The cabin heat was spotty. And the first night's fajr alarm failed.

But no one complained. Because the bar wasn't perfection. It was presence.

They spent the first day in quiet. Reading. Walking. Praying on blankets spread across pine needles and fallen leaves.

At night, they gathered around a small fire made with borrowed wood and whispered du'as.

Musa led a dhikr circle beneath the stars. The silence after the last "Ya Allah" felt like God had bent down to listen.

The second night, they shared stories. No script. Just a question: "What brought you to Islam—or what almost took you from it?"

Amira spoke first. She talked about her parents' divorce. About being the girl who wore hijab at school and still got called fake.

"I thought maybe I didn't belong anywhere. Then I came to Columbia. And one night... I sat in the back of a room while you all spoke honesty into a mic. And I thought... maybe this is what belonging feels like."

Jawad followed. He spoke about addiction. Not his. His brother's. And the guilt of surviving grief while still fasting.

Abe went next. No jokes this time. Just the story of a night he nearly left

Islam in high school. And how a voice note from a brother who barely knew him saved his faith for one more day. "That voice? It was you, Musa. You probably forgot. I didn't."

Musa looked down. Didn't reply. But tears tracked silently down his face.

Tariq didn't plan to speak. But as the firelight cracked and flickered, he looked around the circle.

At Michael holding back emotion.

At Amira with her eyes closed.

At Musa gripping his prayer beads like a lifeline.

At Abe, no longer performing.

And he said: "I came to college to be something great.

Then I realized greatness isn't loud. It's consistent. It's soft. It's honest when no one claps. It's praying Maghrib in the woods with fifteen students who believed you were worth following—not because you had answers, but because you were still asking the right questions."

No one clapped. They just sat. And watched the fire. And felt—held.

That night, after everyone went to sleep, Tariq stayed up. Watched the last coals dim to red.

Opened his notebook and wrote:

> *We were never the fire. We were just the match. The next flame*
> *has caught. And it will burn softer—but longer.*

Chapter Fourteen

Losing the Thread

The First Absence

It started small. A missed message. Then two.

A missed prayer in the lounge. Then a week without showing up.

Michael was the first to ask. "Anyone heard from Abe?"

Tariq looked up from his notebook.

Rohan glanced at his phone.

Musa just shook his head.

"No texts?" Tariq asked.

"Read receipts, no replies," Michael said. "His room's been dark for days."

Musa added quietly: "He hasn't opened my last du'a voice note either."

That was when it became real. They didn't panic. Not yet. They gave it space.

Abe was Abe. Loud. Intense. Prone to withdrawing and reappearing with a new idea or a half-written rap about resilience. But this time felt... heavier.

On Thursday, Michael knocked on Abe's door. No answer. He pressed his ear to the frame.

Music—barely audible. Old Nas. Something from Illmatic. Michael left

175

a note. No reply.

Friday came. The Circle met for Jummah. No Abe. No excuse. No forwarded flyer for a new event. No reposts. Just silence.

Later that day, they sat in the lounge. Tariq stared at the wall. "He's unraveling. And we don't know why."

Rohan: "He's been quiet since the retreat."

Michael: "Maybe seeing people find their own spark scared him."

Musa: "Or maybe he's tired of carrying fire."

Tariq stood. "I'll go see him."

That night, he walked to Abe's room. Knocked. No answer. He waited. Then knocked again.

Finally, the door opened—just a crack. Abe. Eyes bloodshot. Not crying—just worn.

The room behind him was dark, cluttered.

Tariq didn't try to peek in. He just said: "I miss you, bro."

Abe looked down. Then said, voice low: "I don't know how to be useful anymore."

Tariq exhaled. "You don't have to be. Just be here. That's enough."

Abe nodded once. Didn't open the door wider. Didn't close it either.

Tariq stood there for another minute. Then said: "We're praying Isha at 9. If you can't come, we'll still pray for you."

Then he walked away. That night, Abe didn't show. But a chair was left open. And they prayed like he was there.

Tariq's journal:

> *Sometimes the thread doesn't snap. It just slips from your hand when you're not looking. And the question becomes: Will we chase it? Or will we pretend it was never ours to hold?*

The Tension Beneath

The Circle still met. Weekly. On time. Technically. But something had shifted.

The gatherings had gone from sacred to scheduled. Even the salaams felt thinner.

On Tuesday night, the meeting started with logistics. Michael opened his laptop. "We need to decide who's handling Ramadan prep. The masjid wants help organizing the student iftar calendar."

Rohan was sipping tea. Calm. Efficient. "I can do it. I already started drafting a shared doc."

Michael raised an eyebrow. "You didn't think to mention that?"

Rohan blinked. "It's just logistics."

Michael closed the laptop. Not hard—but not gentle either. "It's not just logistics. This isn't a startup."

Rohan's voice stayed level. "You think planning in advance is a problem?"

"No," Michael said. "But acting alone is."

Tariq looked up from the floor. "Yo. What are we actually fighting about?"

Michael leaned back. "I just feel like we've stopped asking each other before we move. We used to be a Circle Now it's project leads and side missions."

Rohan folded his arms. "And I feel like every time I try to keep things from falling apart, someone tells me I'm controlling."

Musa cleared his throat. Soft. Measured. "Maybe we've forgotten the difference between authority and intention."

They fell silent. Not awkwardly. But like the words had sunk too deep to retrieve right away.

Afterward, they stayed behind one by one. Tariq lingered with Michael in the hallway. "You okay?"

Michael exhaled. "I just feel like I'm holding everyone's emotional weight. And when I finally speak, I'm the problem."

Tariq put a hand on his shoulder. "You're not the problem. You're the mirror. And sometimes mirrors scare us."

Downstairs, Rohan sat with Musa. The tea was cold now. Neither of them spoke for a long time.

Then Rohan finally said: "You ever feel like... you're not supposed to be the leader, but if you don't move, nothing happens?"

Musa looked at him. Nodded once. Then said: "But moving without du'a is just... noise."

Rohan looked down. "I haven't made real du'a in weeks."

Musa smiled sadly. "Then let's start there."

That night, in the lounge, Musa stayed behind. Alone.

He vacuumed. Reorganized the books. Wiped the prayer mat clean. Taped up a torn flyer. Then he prayed two long rak'ahs.

Not because he felt holy. But because someone had to guard the stillness.

Tariq's journal:

> *It's easy to track what we've built. Harder to notice what we've buried. Tonight I saw tension carried in silence, frustration masquerading as order, and prayer offered as apology. The Circle is still alive. But right now, it's limping.*

A Conversation Not Had

The text came at 1:46 a.m.

Abe: "You up?"

Tariq was. Not because he couldn't sleep—but because he hadn't even tried. He'd been staring at the ceiling, thinking about silence, pressure, and whether brotherhood still held when no one knew what to say.

Tariq: Yeah. You good?

Abe: Come outside.

They met on the stone steps behind the engineering building. Cold air. No words at first.

Abe was hooded up, hands in pockets, pacing like someone rehearsing the courage to start.

Tariq waited. Didn't push. Finally, Abe sat. Didn't look over.

Just said: "I feel like I'm breaking in places I didn't know could even exist."

Tariq stayed quiet.

Abe continued. "You ever give everything to something... and then wake up one day and realize it didn't fill the hole it promised to?" He looked down.

"The Circle was my mosque, my therapy, my clout, my safe place, my purpose—all of it. And now, even when I'm in the room... I feel like a ghost."

Tariq nodded slowly. "That's real. But ghosts don't text at 1:46 asking someone to come sit in the cold."

Abe cracked a tired smile. "Maybe I'm just a loud ghost." Then: "I stopped coming around because I didn't want y'all to see me unravel. I thought maybe if I just disappeared, I could fix it alone. Come back new. Clean."

Tariq looked at him. Soft. Unflinching. "But love doesn't require polish. Just presence."

Abe blinked hard. Then said something he hadn't even told himself: "I started having panic attacks. One after the retreat. Another after we declined the summit invite. Then again the day Hasan wrote us. I kept thinking... what if I'm the only one who doesn't know how to grow?"

Tariq exhaled. "You're not."

Abe looked over for the first time. Eyes glossy. Exposed.

"Then why does everyone else look like they've figured it out?"

Tariq replied: "Because we've all become better at hiding what we're surviving."

They sat there until the campus lights dimmed to power-save mode. Two silhouettes in the dark. Not healed. But heard.

Before they stood to leave, Abe asked: "You think they still want me back?"

Tariq smiled. "We didn't build this to be a stage. We built it to be a circle. And the thing about a circle..."

He paused.

"There's always space."

In his journal that night, Tariq wrote:

> *Some brothers drift because they're lost. Some drift because they don't want to stain the place they helped build. But tonight, Abe let me see the thread. And even in the unraveling... he held it.*

The Ones Who Stay

He came back on a Wednesday. Not with an announcement. No speech. No group message.

Just walked into the lounge mid-afternoon with a hoodie half-zipped and a bag of mango-flavored sparkling water.

Musa saw him first. Didn't speak. Just nodded. Michael gave a quick dap. Abe returned it—light, but with both palms.

Rohan raised an eyebrow.

Abe shrugged. "I got thirsty. Y'all were the only ones who knew my brand."

Tariq walked in a few minutes later. Saw Abe sitting on the edge of the couch, feet tapping softly.

"Took you long enough," he said.

Abe smirked. "You said there'd be space. Didn't say how awkward it'd feel stepping back into it."

They both laughed. The tension broke like a brittle branch. The meeting that day was simple. Michael read through a few logistics.

Rohan handed out printed materials for the upcoming Ramadan prep.

Musa distributed dates. No one asked Abe to speak. And he didn't try to lead. He just sat. Offered to help draft an email.

Then stayed after to vacuum. Silently. Gently. Like someone sweeping not just crumbs—but shame.

Later that night, Tariq and Abe sat on the dorm rooftop. The wind was louder than their conversation. But it didn't matter. Abe finally said: "You know what's wild? I kept thinking I had to come back and earn it all again. Be the life. Be the hype. Be the voice."

He paused. "But y'all didn't ask for any of that. You just left the seat open."

Tariq nodded. "We never wanted a mascot. We wanted a mirror."

In the masjid that week, Abe made du'a out loud for the first time since the retreat. Not poetic. Not perfect. Just three words, whispered into sujood: "Ya Allah, keep me."

The Circle didn't post anything. No updates. No celebratory pictures. Just five brothers—again—gathered on a carpet. Still cracked. Still healing. Still showing up.

Tariq's journal:

> *The ones who stay aren't the ones with answers. They're the ones who choose not to run— even when they're limping. And maybe that's enough.*

The Thread We Hold

There was no agenda that Friday. No Google Doc. No flyer. No upcoming event to plan for. Just a quiet invite in the group chat from Michael:

Michael: "Let's meet. Nothing heavy. Just tea, prayer, and breath."

No one replied with words. But by 7:15 p.m., they were all there. Tariq, Rohan, Michael, Musa, Abe. Five chairs in a circle. Two thermoses of tea. One candle on the floor—flickering with no symbolism, just soft light.

They didn't start with prayer. They started with silence. Comfortable now. Not like before, when silence felt like decay. Now, it felt like healing.

Tariq finally spoke.

"I've been thinking a lot about thread."

They looked at him.

"How easy it is to lose. How hard it is to knot again. But also… how sometimes, it's the softest things that hold the strongest weight."

Musa nodded. "Like sincerity."

Rohan added: "Like forgiveness."

Abe looked around. "Like just showing up when you don't know what to say."

Michael leaned back. "Like not quitting—even when you thought you already did."

They all laughed. Softly. Fully.

They didn't make a new plan that night. They didn't write anything down.

But they poured tea for each other. Passed dates.

Prayed two rak'ahs—led by Abe, who paused before Surah Fatiha like he was asking permission from the silence.

And when they finished, no one rushed to leave. They just sat. Like brothers. Like witnesses. Like people who had burned and rebuilt and now just needed to be together.

Before they left, Michael pulled a small piece of red thread from his pocket. Held it up. "I found this in my jacket the day after the retreat," he said. "I don't know how it got there."

He placed it on the center table. Left it there. No one asked for meaning.

They just nodded. Like it belonged. Tariq's journal that night:

We didn't fix everything. We didn't return to what we were. But we gathered. And sometimes, gathering is the most sacred act. The thread is not tight. But it's still in our hands.

CHAPTER FIFTEEN

What Forgiveness Requires

The Ghost We Let In

It began with a flyer. Slipped under dorm doors. Tacked to bulletin boards. Shared on stories.

Black text on a pale green background: "Justice for Bilal — We Demand Transparency." A teach-in. A sit-down. A reckoning. Monday, 7PM. Hart Auditorium.

The Circle saw it the same way they all remembered him. Quick. Raw. Unfinished. Bilal wasn't a friend. But he was a shadow.

A Muslim student who had once been part of the broader MSA community. Who spoke too much, laughed too loud, and challenged things nobody wanted to touch—racism in prayer spaces, classism in student organizing, silence around Palestine, stigma around mental health.

Then one day—he disappeared. Rumors flew. Suspension? Harassment? Grades? No answers. Just silence. And a reputation that turned into a myth.

That was freshman year. Now, he was back.

The Circle didn't talk about it the first two days. But everyone felt it.

It wasn't until Sunday night, in the lounge, that Michael finally said: "We let it happen."

The words hit like cold water.

Tariq looked up. "What do you mean?"

Michael's voice was quiet. "We saw him unraveling. Loudly. Publicly. And we just... let him go. Because he was inconvenient. Too messy for our neat little image."

Musa sat back. "He was also reckless. He called people out without knowing full context. Stirred chaos. Sometimes cruelty."

Abe added, "Yeah, he burned every bridge he touched."

Tariq stayed silent. Then said: "But were those bridges worth protecting... if they only led back to our own comfort?"

Silence. Musa frowned. "So what do you want? To apologize? To bring him back into the Circle?"

"No," Tariq said. "I want us to tell the truth. Even if it's too late."

That Monday, they attended the teach-in. Not as speakers. Not as guests of honor. Just students. Sitting in the back row. Listening.

Bilal was there.

Not on stage. Not at the mic. Just sitting cross-legged on the floor with a small group of first-year students, nodding gently as others shared their stories.

One speaker—Amira—spoke about silence in Muslim spaces.

"How we pretend inclusion while protecting hierarchies. How we gaslight vulnerability. How we uplift the polished and disappear the raw."

Tariq felt every syllable like it was carved from his own ribs.

After the event, Musa walked out first. Tariq followed. They ended up by the campus fountain—half-lit, draped in the buzz of streetlights.

Musa finally turned to him. "You think we failed him."

Tariq shook his head. "I think we failed ourselves—by pretending someone else's messiness meant they didn't deserve compassion."

Musa folded his arms. "Forgiveness can't exist without repentance. He never owned anything."

Tariq nodded. "Maybe. But maybe we don't forgive to exonerate. Maybe we forgive so we don't rot."

That night, Tariq journaled:

> *Forgiveness is not forgetting. It is the soft decision to carry*
> *less weight. And tonight, I carried Bilal's name back into my*
> *prayers. Not because he deserved it. But because I needed the*
> *room.*

Grace Like Gravity

It wasn't a teach-in or a protest. It was the halal cart behind Hamilton Hall. Wednesday night. Rain whispering on pavement.

Musa wanted lentil soup. Tariq tagged along. Neither of them expected anyone else to be there.

But Bilal was standing in line. Umbrella over one shoulder. Hands in coat pockets. Hoodie half-zipped. His posture wasn't defensive. It was... light. As if he had finally stopped carrying the whole world on his back.

He saw them. And didn't flinch. Didn't smile. Just nodded once.

Tariq didn't think. He just stepped forward. "Bilal."

Bilal turned fully. "Tariq."

Musa stayed behind. Watching.

The space between them wasn't wide. But it held years.

Tariq searched for the right words. Found none.

So he started with the truth. "I didn't stand up for you."

Bilal raised an eyebrow. "When?"

"When you were unraveling. When you said things that made us uncomfortable. When people started calling you unstable instead of honest."

Bilal said nothing.

So Tariq continued. "You didn't always say it right. But you were trying. And we let you fall alone."

Bilal exhaled. "You think a five-minute conversation makes up for two years of being invisible?"

Tariq shook his head. "No. I think five minutes of truth can sometimes do what two years of silence never could."

Another pause. Then Bilal said: "You know what hurt most? I wasn't mad at y'all. I expected it. I expected to be left."

Tariq felt that one in his spine.

Bilal added: "What surprised me was how long it took me to realize I still needed to forgive you. Not because you asked. Just because I didn't want to carry you in my chest anymore like glass."

Musa stepped forward then. Softly.

"You still pray?"

Bilal nodded.

"More now than I ever did before. Softer. Smaller. Less show, more need."

Musa smiled faintly. "Then we're still family. Even if we broke."

Bilal didn't smile. But his eyes shifted.

The tension dissolved—not completely, but gently. They didn't hug. No tears. No dramatic reconciliations.

Just three Muslim men, standing under dim light, while a halal vendor filled plastic containers behind them.

As they walked away, Tariq whispered: "That wasn't closure."

Musa replied: "No. That was compassion. And sometimes, that's heavier."

Tariq's journal that night:

> *We met again. Not to mend. Just to name the distance. And I realized...Grace isn't floating above someone's pain. It's standing in it with them. Quietly. Without a rope. Just presence. Just gravity.*

The Prayer We Needed

It wasn't on the calendar. No one scheduled it. No message in the group chat. But one by one, they showed up—Wednesday night, after the Bilal encounter.

Tariq arrived first.

Then Michael.

Then Abe, carrying prayer mats under one arm and his usual noise tucked far behind his ribs.

Musa came in last, holding nothing but a thermos of tea and the kind of calm that said, Allah has already forgiven things you haven't even named yet.

They laid the mats in a wide semi-circle.

No one spoke. No one asked, Who's leading?

They just began. The first rak'ah was slow. The second slower. By the third, some were weeping.

Not because of guilt. But because they were tired of carrying what wasn't theirs anymore.

After they prayed, they didn't break the silence. Tariq finally whispered: "Let's make du'a together."

No fancy words. No Arabic-heavy prelude. Just heartbeats translated into breath.

Michael spoke first: "Ya Allah, make space in us for people we've given up on."

Abe followed: "Forgive the parts of me that clung to performance instead of presence."

Rohan: "Help me lead without needing credit."

Musa: "Replace my pride with patience."

Tariq closed: "And if this Circle is still pleasing to You, preserve it. Not in numbers. Not in clout. But in sincerity."

They sat after the du'a. Still on the floor. Still half-wrecked, half-reborn.

No plans. No next steps. Just light in their chests and dust in their mouths.

Outside, the wind picked up. And inside, it felt like the air had cleared.

Not because everything was resolved. But because they had stopped hiding from the God who already knew it all.

Tariq's journal that night:

> *Tonight we prayed like boys who stopped pretending they were men. We prayed like men who knew they were still learning how to love. We didn't ask to be better. We asked to be real. And that was enough.*

Something Still Burning

A week passed. No crisis. No announcements. Just quiet growth.

The lounge was still theirs. The thread was still intact. But something had shifted—not away, but within.

Tariq sat on the rooftop again. Same spot. Same wind. Only now, it didn't feel like he was searching for God.

It felt like he was remembering Him.

Michael was prepping for a panel on tech and ethics.

Abe had agreed to speak at a high school youth circle—not because he had answers, but because he had honesty.

Musa was meeting with a new convert every Wednesday night for Qur'an and tea.

Rohan had taken a break from planning—to listen more.

And Tariq? He was writing again. Not speeches. Letters. To his future self. To his sister. To Hasan. To Bilal. To the fire that once felt like burden, now revealed as light.

One night, they all met up for tea. No agenda. No mission. Just laughter. Reminiscing. Soft plans for Eid break.

The conversation turned to the future. Who would graduate when. Where people might move. What would happen to the Circle. Abe asked it first: "So... when we're gone... what happens to this?"

Musa sipped his tea. Smiled. "Maybe it becomes a memory."

Michael added: "Or a seed."

Tariq looked around. "Or maybe it already became what it needed to. A room. A rug. A reason to stay faithful. And maybe that's enough."

No one disagreed.

Because no one needed to.

Later that night, Tariq journaled:

> *We kept trying to protect the fire. But it was never ours to own. It belongs to the ones who light it next. And the ones after them. As long as someone, somewhere, kneels to pray in a quiet room— something we built still burns.*

CHAPTER SIXTEEN

The Circle We Made

The Letter They'll Never Read

Bismillah.

I don't know your name. I don't know your major. Or your skin color. Or what city you'll come from when you arrive here.

I don't know what will break your heart the first semester. Or what will keep you from breaking apart when everything else does.

But I do know this: There will come a night when you'll wonder why you ever thought you belonged.

Maybe you'll walk out of a Friday prayer in silence, feeling like no one looked you in the eye.

Maybe you'll sit in a masjid event and feel like you're too liberal, too Black, too confused, too visible.

Maybe you'll watch your faith leak slowly out of your chest in lectures and parties and WhatsApp groups where people quote Islam but forget mercy.

Maybe you'll miss home.

Or maybe you'll be relieved to be far from it—and then feel guilty about that too.

You'll get tired. Of performance. Of piety that feels performative. Of

191

pressure to be the "good Muslim" your family, your campus, your ummah want you to be.

But listen—don't leave.

Or if you do, leave for a little while.

Cry in stairwells. Skip an MSA meeting. Delete Instagram for a week. Lay in your bed and whisper to a Lord you're not sure is still listening.

But then... come back.

Even if your du'a is dry. Even if your prayer is quiet. Even if your beard is gone or your hijab is slipping or your heart is louder than your iman.

Come back.

Because what we built was never about perfection. It was about presence.

We weren't perfect either. We were a bunch of boys with egos and trauma and jokes we used to hide our insecurities. We made flyers with typos. We argued over who should lead salah. We forgot each other's birthdays and du'a lists.

But we prayed together.

We forgave badly—but we forgave. We told the truth out loud—even when it broke the room open. We didn't go viral. But we survived.

And sometimes, that's the revolution.

So if you're reading this somehow—because someone found it in a drawer, or passed it around in a group chat, or left it printed behind in a campus masjid—

I'm not asking you to rebuild what we made. I'm asking you to build what's needed now. Leave your own warmth. Make your own circle. Even if it starts with one rug.

One voice. One whisper in the night.

We didn't make a movement. We made a space.

A place to breathe. A place to fall apart and still be loved. A place to pray without performance.

Make that again. Make it better. Make it yours.

And if you ever forget how— just sit down. Say bismillah. And listen to who's still willing to stay.

The New Flame

It happened on a Tuesday. A quiet one.

Clouds low over the quad. Leaves already turning. Campus in that early-fall state between stress and solitude.

Tariq was exiting the prayer room when a small voice called after him. "Hey—Brother Tariq, right?"

He turned. Three students stood there. Wide-eyed. Nervous.

He recognized one from last semester's retreat. Amira's cousin.

The others? New. New to the Circle. New to Columbia. New to... something else, too. The kind of new that held both awe and ache.

"We were wondering," one began, "if the Circle still... meets?"

Tariq blinked. Then smiled. "Define 'meets.'"

One of them laughed nervously.

"We heard stories. About open mics. Dhikr nights. That rooftop du'a? People say it shifted something in the air. We've been looking for something like that. Something real."

Tariq nodded slowly. "We still gather. Sometimes. When the soul needs it."

They hesitated. "Would it be okay if we... sat in sometime?"

Tariq looked up at the sky. Soft clouds. No sunlight. Just peace.

"It's not ours anymore," he said. "It's everyone's. Just bring your full self. That's the only price of admission."

That night, the Circle met. Not all of them. But enough.

Musa brought candles.

Michael brought ginger tea.

Abe printed out old poems and handed them out like scripture.

Rohan, now quieter than ever, simply greeted each newcomer by name.

"Salaam, I'm glad you're here."

No hierarchy. No mic. Just people sitting cross-legged on a rug, learning how to be before trying to teach.

Tariq stayed back as they began. Watched as one of the new students asked how to pronounce a line from Qur'an. Watched as Musa guided him softly, without performance. Watched as Michael offered dates and someone cried into their tea and no one made it weird.

It wasn't replication. It was resurrection. A new version of the Circle.

One that didn't need to remember names. Only presence.

Later, as they cleaned up, one of the freshmen turned to Tariq.

"So... what's your role now?"

Tariq paused. Then said: "I'm just a witness now. I built the first fire. But this one? This one's yours."

Tariq's journal that night:

> *This wasn't about legacy. It was about making room. And tonight, we didn't just pass the flame. We proved it never needed protecting. Just permission.*

The Last Circle

The invitation was simple. A group text. No flyer. No countdown.

Tariq: "Let's meet. One last time. Same place we started."

Saturday night. 8:47 p.m. Same lounge. Same rug.

Tariq arrived first. Lit a single candle in the center.

Then came Michael—with a new thermos, a little dented, filled with ginger clove chai.

Then Abe—carrying a Bluetooth speaker he didn't even plug in. "No playlist tonight," he said. "Just memories."

Rohan followed, quieter than usual, eyes soft, holding a small envelope. He didn't mention it.

And finally, Musa. No fanfare. Just a salaam and a hug that held a thousand unsaid things.

They sat in a loose circle again. Not like freshmen now. Like men who had survived each other.

Tariq spoke first. "I've been thinking about beginnings."

Michael smiled. "We didn't even know how to fold a prayer mat back then."

Abe added, "Or how to stop talking over each other."

Musa: "Or how to say 'I'm sorry' out loud."

They laughed. But gently. Then came the part they hadn't planned. One by one, they spoke. What they had held in for years.

Michael: "I didn't always know how to be soft. I masked it with structure. Planning. Control. But this Circle made me softer. Gave me permission."

Rohan: "I regret how much I let my need to prove myself cost me presence. I led with performance. I should've led with love."

Abe: "I thought I had to entertain y'all to be worthy. But you stayed even when I stopped being loud. That means more than I ever said."

Musa: "I came in with Qur'an and discipline, thinking that was all I had to give. But y'all showed me the power of being broken and still loved."

Tariq last: "I thought I was the glue. But it turns out... the glue was all of us. And maybe the Circle was never meant to last forever. Just long enough to make sure we didn't lose ourselves."

Then Rohan handed each of them an envelope.

Inside: a printed photo.

Their first meeting. MSA orientation. Five kids on a dorm floor, smiling like they had no idea what they were building. They didn't. That was the miracle. No one cried. They just breathed. Prayed two *rak'ahs*.

Then sat in silence. A silence that held weight, warmth, and witness. They didn't say goodbye. They didn't need to.

Tariq's journal:

The Circle didn't end. It expanded beyond its shape. Tonight, we didn't close a chapter. We honored a heartbeat. And in sha Allah, that beat will echo in rooms we'll never enter— through names we'll never know.

CHAPTER SEVENTEEN

The Fire They Found

New Names, Same Light

They didn't call themselves The Circle. They called it "Safar." Arabic for "journey."

Not arrival. Not victory. Just movement.

The name came from a sophomore who had sat in the back of one of the last gatherings, scribbling lines in a notebook that never left her side.

The space was smaller now. Not the big campus lounge. But a borrowed prayer room in the chemistry building. Slightly musty. Soft carpet. No windows.

And still, the light was there. Not overhead. Within.

Tariq visited once a month. No speeches. No mentoring plan. Just presence.

He sat near the back, quietly sipping tea and listening as new students shared the weight they were carrying:

"My father's proud of my grades but not my faith."

"I don't know if I'm Muslim enough to belong here."

"I'm afraid that if I speak my truth, I'll lose my place in the masjid."

Tariq didn't offer answers. He offered listening.

Musa taught Qur'an sometimes. But only when asked.

Michael built a shared digital archive of old writings, poems, flyers, even voice notes from retreats past. He called it "Legacy Without Ego."

Abe? He mentored high schoolers in Harlem now. Came back only when they asked him to perform a poem. Always cried after.

Rohan watched from afar. He sent donations. Brought fruit. Checked in. He was building something else now: a family. Married. Expecting. Still Rohan. Just... expanded.

The new students didn't need them every day.

That was the point.

They had each other. And that, somehow, made the Circle feel eternal.

One day, after a gathering, a first-year sister asked Tariq a question: "What do we owe the ones who came before?"

He smiled. "Nothing."

Then paused.

"Except to be as honest as they were. Or maybe... more."

He walked back to his dorm that night with Musa. Neither spoke until they reached the steps. Then Musa said: "It lasted."

Tariq nodded. "Longer than I ever thought it could."

Musa smiled. "Maybe it's not fire. Maybe it's light. Fire fades. Light lingers."

That night, Tariq journaled:

> *I used to think legacy meant your name on a wall. Now I think it's your du'a echoing in a room you're no longer in. They found the fire. But more importantly—they're keeping it soft. And that's the kind of light that survives.*

The Last Goodbye

Musa was leaving. Not just the university. The country. A fellowship had come through—Qur'anic manuscript preservation in Istanbul.

A dream. A calling. A long-awaited whisper answered after years of stillness.

He announced it without fanfare. In the group chat.

Musa: "I leave end of the month, in sha Allah. Would love to pray with you all one more time before I go."

That was it. No speeches. Just presence.

They gathered on the rooftop again.

No mic. No circle name. No "event."

Just five brothers under the early spring stars.

Michael brought dates.

Rohan brought tea.

Abe brought a printed list of old Circle quotes—he read none of them.

Tariq brought his full heart.

Musa brought his *tasbih*.

They prayed two *rak'ahs*.

In silence. Musa led. Slow. Measured. Each verse felt like soil being turned, seeds being buried, ready for new light.

After prayer, no one moved.

Tariq finally spoke. "You were our compass."

Musa smiled. "I was just the one who remembered where *Qiblah* was when y'all were arguing about GPS."

Laughter. Then stillness again. Rohan handed him a small pouch. Inside: an old key. To the lounge. The one they'd all copied, passed around, lost, and found again over the years. "We figured... someone should carry it. Even if the door changes."

Musa held it tight.

Abe stepped forward next. "I thought you'd leave with a quote. A speech. A memory."

Musa shook his head. "No. I want to leave with a du'a."

He turned toward the city skyline. Whispered:

Ya Allah... make them softer than they want to be, stronger than they know how to be, and braver than they believe they can be. Let them forget me. But let them never forget the light we kept alive.

Tears fell. No one wiped theirs. There was no shame here. They hugged him, one by one. Not to hold him. But to release him.

As Musa disappeared down the stairwell for the last time, no one chased after him.

Tariq just whispered: "That's how you know it was love. You can let it go. And it still burns."

That night, he wrote:

Musa left quietly. But everything he touched still echoes. We didn't bury him in memory. We planted him in the future.

Something Holy Left Behind

The pouch was found the following Friday. Not by Tariq. Not by Michael. By Kareem—one of the new students.

He'd been rearranging prayer mats in the lounge when he saw it. Tucked beneath the old bookshelf. Wrapped in a white cloth. Tied with a cord of *misbaha* beads.

He opened it slowly. Inside: a journal. Unlabeled. Weathered leather. No ornament.

Just pages and pages of du'as, poems, Qur'an reflections, and quiet notes—from Musa. Some dated. Some not. Some written in Arabic. Some in aching, unfiltered English.

A page was marked with a torn post-it note. On it, one sentence: *"This Circle was never mine. I just watered it until the roots held."*

They brought it to Tariq. He opened it. Read two pages. Then closed it, kissed the cover, and whispered, "SubhanAllah."

That night, they didn't gather to discuss it. They just gathered.

Michael read a du'a.

Abe brought back the poem he had once performed and never recited again.

Rohan offered water.

No one tried to turn it into an event. They just sat in it. The weight. The peace. The presence.

Later, Tariq opened the journal again. Found another note, scribbled in the margin of a reflection on Surah Al-Hujurat: *"You won't always be remembered. But you can always choose to be light."*

He smiled. Then cried. Not with grief. With completion.

In his final entry for the evening, Tariq wrote:

> *We keep looking for holy in loud places. But sometimes, holy is tucked under a bookshelf. Left behind by someone who prayed more than he posted. Something sacred lives here now. Not in our names. But in the stillness we protected.*

Chapter Eighteen

What We Left Lit

Before the End Begins

The graduation robe arrived in a thin, clear plastic bag—folded like a grocery-store tablecloth, creased at every angle.

Tariq opened it slowly, like it might dissolve in his hands.

He laid it across the bed in silence. Dark blue. Gold trim. A collar that tried to make polyester look noble.

It wasn't the robe itself that froze him. It was what it symbolized—a closing door. An old identity being folded, quietly, into the past.

His room looked almost the same as it had freshman year. Same wooden desk. Same cracked closet mirror. Same view of the library steps.

But something about the air felt... older.

Or maybe it was him.

The books on the shelf weren't about law school anymore. They were about grief, masculinity, community healing, Islamic psychology.

The bulletin board held photos now—Musa at the retreat. Abe sleeping with his face half-covered by a notebook. A post-it with Michael's handwriting: "Silence is still a form of love if you hold it gently."

Tariq stared at the photos and whispered: "We were just boys. And now..."

He didn't finish. Didn't have to. The phone rang just after Maghrib. His father.

Still firm. Still measuring life in metrics—degrees, careers, long-term plans.

"We're proud of you, son. You made it."

Tariq smiled into the phone.

"Thanks, Baba."

But in his chest, the reply was different:

"I haven't made it. I'm still making it. And the man I became is not the one you imagined—but he's finally someone I recognize."

He took a walk. No destination. Just footsteps echoing against the quiet architecture of memory.

The quad was mostly empty—finals week done, students scattered.

He walked past the stone wall where Musa had once recited Surah Al-Asr beneath a full moon, and no one dared breathe.

Past the old dorm where he and Rohan argued at 2 a.m. over justice and pragmatism.

Past the small masjid annex where Amira had once cried into her palms, and Michael offered her tea without saying a word.

Each step felt like rereading a chapter out loud with no intention of rewriting it.

A warm breeze moved through the trees, stirring early summer pollen into lazy spirals of gold. Tariq paused by the science building and noticed a flyer taped crookedly to the wall. SAFAR PRESENTS: RAMADAN REFLECTIONS A Night of Stories, Du'a, and Belonging.

The font was new. The logo different. None of the names listed were familiar. He smiled. Not because he was needed. But because he wasn't.

He stopped near the fountain. Sat on the cold rim. Listened. Not to water. To silence. And in that stillness, something became crystal clear: They had never built a legacy to keep their names alive. They had built it so someone else's name could breathe without fear.

His phone buzzed.

A message from Abe.

Abe: "One last rooftop? Just us?"

Tariq: "Always."

Later, before leaving his room, he opened his journal and wrote:

> *The fire doesn't follow you. If you lit it right, it stays behind—*
> *warming hands you'll never see. Graduation isn't the crown.*
> *It's the moment you realize… you don't need one.*

Caps and Candles

They met on the rooftop—unannounced. No RSVP. No flyer. No shared Google Doc like years before. Just a message from Tariq: "Tonight. Same roof. Bring your breath."

The sun was already dropping behind the skyline when they arrived.

Michael brought mint tea and silence.

Rohan brought a folded kufi and the last copy of his undergraduate thesis, marked with red ink and dried jasmine petals.

Abe came with nothing but a white hoodie and the same crooked grin he wore their first week on campus.

Tariq brought candles. Ten of them. The kind you light for mood, not mourning. But tonight, it felt like both.

They spread out an old tapestry—faded, frayed on the corners. Musa had once called it "the carpet of mercy."

Musa wasn't here now. But his absence wasn't felt as lack. It was felt as legacy. His journal sat between them, closed. A bookmark tucked at a page that simply read: "Let light be the language you leave behind."

They sat cross-legged, knees touching. Each brother placed something at the center of the circle.

Michael, a pen. "The one I used to write the letter I never sent to my mom."

Rohan, a small string of black tasbih. "Given to me by a stranger on a bus during finals week. I kept it when I didn't feel worthy of holding anything holy."

Abe, a folded piece of paper. "A list of the names I prayed for when I couldn't pray for myself."

Tariq, a matchbook. "The last one from the original Circle retreat. I lit a candle with it the night I finally told my father I wouldn't go to law school."

They didn't explain why they were offering these things. They just laid them down like truths.

The breeze was warm but unsure. City lights blinked like slow du'as from buildings too tired to speak.

Tariq leaned back on his palms and looked up. "You ever think about what we almost became?"

Michael nodded. "Influencers. Organizers. The 'good Muslim boys' everyone reposted."

Abe laughed softly. "Alhamdulillah for failure."

They laughed with him. Then fell into quiet.

They prayed Isha without choosing a leader.

No one stood first. They simply rose together. Moved as one. A circle not of boys anymore, but men with softened edges and full hearts. The kind of men who didn't lead with certainty, but with witness.

After prayer, they stayed seated. Not because they had more to say. But because there was nothing left that required words.

Abe lit one candle. Passed the flame to Michael. Who passed it to Rohan. Who passed it to Tariq.

Tariq placed the flame at the center.

One candle, surrounded by shadows and breath.

"We didn't become legends," he said.

Michael replied: "We became light."

In Tariq's journal that night, his final entry before walking across the stage read:

> *Tonight, I didn't feel the end. I felt the middle we left in safe hands. The candle wasn't bright. But it stayed lit. And that's the only proof I ever needed.*

What We Were Never Meant to Keep

The morning after the rooftop gathering, the lounge was quiet.

No one planned to meet.

But one by one, they came.

Not for prayer.

Not for ritual.

Just... to leave things behind.

Michael was first.

He sat cross-legged in the corner with a box in his lap. Inside: three worn notebooks filled with early meeting notes, scribbled logistics, pages of ideas they never had time—or courage—to implement.

He opened the first one, flipped to a random page.

"Host a MSA Fast-A-Thon featuring community voices, not just popular scholars."

He smiled.

Closed it.

Set it on the table near the bookshelf.

No announcement. Just a quiet goodbye.

Rohan came next.

He brought a plastic folder—sealed, weather-worn.

Inside: rejection letters. Six of them. From internships, business fellowships, and one that crushed him more than he'd ever admitted.

He placed the folder inside a cardboard sleeve labeled: "Things That Didn't Define Me."

Then sat beside Michael.

Didn't say a word.

Abe came in last.

Wearing black.

No hoodie this time. Just jeans and an old retreat t-shirt he hadn't worn in over a year.

He walked straight to the carpet. Pulled something from his pocket.

A single index card.

On it, written in small black ink:

"I forgive myself for how loud I was when I needed to be heard—and how silent I became when I needed to be loved."

He folded it once. Then again.

Placed it beneath the corner of the prayer mat.

"No one needs to see it," he said.

Michael nodded.

"But someone might feel it."

Tariq came later. Alone.

He didn't bring paper. Or photos. Or memories.

He brought his phone.

Opened the "Voice Notes" folder he had kept since freshman year— du'as, ideas, confessions, sermons he never gave, recordings of late-night thoughts he didn't have the strength to write down.

"I used to think documenting meant preserving legacy," he whispered.

Then deleted the folder. All of it.

"Now I think it just meant I was afraid I'd be forgotten."

He looked up. Smiled.

"I don't need to be remembered. Just reflected."

They stayed in the lounge for hours. Not building anything new.

Just cleaning. Reorganizing the shelf. Sweeping. Watering the one plant they'd managed not to kill.

"This place was never ours," Rohan said. "We just borrowed it long enough to heal."

Before they left, Abe stood by the door and looked back. "So what now?"

Michael smiled. "Now we give it away."

Tariq's journal that night:

> *There are things we were never meant to keep. Pain. Ego. Perfection. Shame. But if we let go with love— what remains is light. Weightless. And waiting for the next hand.*

Afterlight

Time passed like breath. Slow. Unannounced.

Tariq stayed in New York. He didn't go to law school. He took a job working with justice-involved youth in the Bronx. Days spent in courtrooms, rec centers, dusty libraries with cracked windows and chairs that wobbled with truth.

At night, he prayed quieter than before. But deeper.

He journaled less. Laughed more. Grieved gently.

Michael moved to D.C. A tech company hired him for strategy. But by year's end, he was building a spiritual mindfulness app on the side.

"Faith without utility," he said. "That's the dream."

He fasted Mondays and Thursdays. Sent voice notes once a week to the group chat—usually reminders, sometimes jokes.

Always signed off with: "Make du'a for me. Even if I haven't said what for."

Rohan got married. To a girl he met through a bookstore fundraiser.

They prayed together in whispers. She taught him how to rest. He taught her how to dream.

They were expecting.

He told the group in a single sentence: "It's a girl. I think I'll name her Safa."

No one questioned it. No one cried. But the thread tugged in all of them.

Abe was all over the map. Spoken word performances in L.A. Workshops in Chicago. School visits in Detroit.

But he always came home for Eid.

"Home," he said, "is where people remember your silence, not just your voice."

They didn't talk every week. Some months, not at all. But the thread held. Tugged. Braided itself through time.

Then came Eid.

Rohan suggested it. A simple gathering. No venue. Just a sunrise walk in Central Park followed by pancakes and prayer rugs on the grass.

Tariq came. Michael brought tea in a thermos so large Abe called it "barakah-sized." Abe brought a new poem and didn't perform it. Just handed it over. Rohan brought his daughter—small, curious, wrapped in pink and wrapped in light.

"She already knows Surah Ikhlas," he said.

Abe whispered, "Of course she does. She was born from sincerity."

They prayed near the water. Birds overhead. Ducks moving like they knew what salah was.

Tariq led. Not because he was first. But because his voice trembled just enough to remind them they were still men who felt.

Afterward, they sat in a loose circle. No candles. No speech. No need.

A child giggled. A breeze passed. And everything felt exactly like it used to.

But also—more.

Tariq's final journal entry:

> *Light doesn't always return in the form it left. Sometimes it comes back softer. Held by new hands. Whispered through new names. But it's still ight. Still the warmth we prayed for.*

The Circle We Left Lit

Bismillah.

I used to think the story needed a clean ending. Some perfect closing chapter. A final prayer. A signature under our names in gold.

But now I know:

Some stories aren't supposed to end. Some are meant to be passed on like tasbih beads, finger to finger. Some are meant to whisper through years in rooms you'll never walk into. Some are meant to leave a single candle lit—and trust that someone else will protect the flame.

We didn't change the world. We didn't fix the ummah. We didn't go viral.

We built a room. We filled it with breath, du'a, laughter, discomfort, tears, mango juice, Qur'an, journals, and silence.

We lit something real.

And real has a way of surviving.

To whoever comes next— You don't need our names. You don't need our stories. You just need your own truth. You need your own room. And someone willing to sit with you in the quiet, until the shame leaves your chest and the light returns to your bones.

If you find this book, this journal, this voice— Don't make it sacred. Make it useful. Break what needs breaking. Build what heals. Keep what burns clean. And never let them tell you your fire must be loud to be holy.

We are gone now. Moved. Married. Raising daughters. Making tea. Writing code. Teaching boys how to pray without fearing their own softness.

But the Circle? It's still lit.

Somewhere. In the pause between adhan and iqamah. In the pages of a freshman's notebook. In the breath a Black Muslim girl exhales when she finds out she's not alone. In the cracked voice of a brother who just said "Ameen" for the first time in weeks.

This is not a goodbye. This is a hand left open. Waiting. Warm. Lit. For you.

Wa salamu alaykum wa rahmatullah.

Wa barakAllahu feekum.

Ameen.

Author's Note

I didn't write this novel to give answers.

I wrote it to hold space.

The Circle We Made is a love letter to Muslim students navigating identity, faith, race, and purpose in a world that often asks them to shrink.

This story is fiction—but the fire behind it is real. The confusion. The brilliance. The heartbreak. The resistance. The joy.

If you see yourself in Tariq, or Musa, or Abe, or anyone else—it's because this story was never just mine to tell.

It was ours.

And it still is.